Alex Jackson: SWA

Pat Flynn teaches at Siena College on Queensland's Sunshine Coast. Before becoming a teacher he was a professional tennis player and coach, travelling the world during the 1980s and 90s.

He loves playing tennis, surfing, skateboarding and figuring out the meaning of life whilst hanging out at the beach.

SWA is a sequel to his very popular first novel for young readers, *Alex Jackson: Grommet*.

Also by Pat Flynn

Alex Jackson: Grommet

ALEX JACKSON

SUKA

Pat Flynn

University of Queensland Press

First published 2002 by University of Queensland Press
Box 6042, St Lucia, Queensland 4067 Australia

www.uqp.uq.edu.au

www.patflynnwriter.com

Typeset by University of Queensland Press
Printed in Australia by McPherson's Printing Group

Distributed in the USA and Canada by
International Specialized Book Services, Inc.,
5824 N.E. Hassalo Street, Portland, Oregon 97213–3640

This project has been assisted by
the Commonwealth Government through
the Australia Council, its arts funding
and advisory body.

Sponsored by the Queensland Office
of Arts and Cultural Development.

Cataloguing in Publication Data
National Library of Australia

Flynn, Patt, 1968–   .
  Alex Jackson: SWA

  1. Skateboarders — Fiction. 2. Teenage boys — Fiction.
  I. Title

A823.4

ISBN 0 7022 3307 2

To Trinity for inspiration
My first readers – Leonie, Liz, Yotta,
Kirrilee, and Cath
Siena College and most of all
My family

Without a board I walk
With it I fly

Julie Tatz

CHAPTER 1
She's Back

Alex Jackson pushed off, felt the rush as he dropped down the smooth concrete bank, and knew once more that all was right with the world. The cool morning air whipped back his blonde hair, and his knees straightened as the concrete levelled out, acting like the accelerator of a hotted-up Torana. He was across the width of the skatepark faster than a Blink 182 song, and as he went over the top of a 2-metre ramp he pulled a manual along the thin path that ran parallel to the drop. He held the wheelie for 5 metres until he rolled back in down the ramp.

At seven in the morning most boarders were sleeping off yesterday's bruises, so Alex and his mate, Casey Marshall, had the Beeton skatepark to themselves. Casey was taking a break from skating the vert ramp and was playing with his latest toy — a Sony digital camera — filming Alex

1

for a skating video he was putting together. In a few minutes Alex would return the favour and become cameraman.

Picking up speed Alex headed for the bank on the west side of the park. As he approached the transition he quickly spun the board 180 degrees and went fakie up the steep incline. He transferred all his weight to his left foot the split second he got to the top, which allowed him to sit in a tail-stall on the metal coping. He rested there for a few seconds, getting ready for the trick that would secure his place on the video — a boardslide down the steep rail connected to the funbox. Of course, when you are in a skating video with Casey Marshall, even a boardslide down a 3-metre rail makes you nothing more than a supporting actor.

Alex reminded himself not to think. Last year when his mind was on other things, he had a series of stacks that left him with an almost permanent headache. But all that had changed. For one thing, there were no longer any girls in his life. Well, there was his mum, of course, his sister, Sam, and his friend, Sarah Sceney — but no *girls*. None who made his heart almost jump out of his chest and his knees shaky. None who kissed him on the mouth while waiting for the train, then took off to Italy before there could be a sequel. None who emailed him every Friday except for the last three — when she had bagged him without an explanation. *She's probably hooked up with some Italian guy*, Alex had decided glumly. Nah, he had no distractions now, and he was skating better than ever.

He leant onto his right foot and dropped back in. Even though it was early morning the January sun warmed his back beneath his baggy white T-shirt. This was the perfect end to the summer holidays. They had started with Alex and his best mate, Jimmy Homan, learning how to surf at the Sunshine Coast. He had shared some quality time with his dad, otherwise known as Chief, down at the Logan City Boxing Club. About a thousand push-ups and punches later, Alex even managed to find some muscles in his arms and chest. And he'd grown three centimetres. He was still small for a 14-year-old, but at least he was now taller than his 12-year-old sister — by the length of a bee's antennae. It would have been the best holiday ever except for …

Don't think.

As he reached the top of the funbox Alex bent down and prepared to ollie. He'd been hesitant with boardslides after he nearly killed himself on this same rail last year, but practising on the flat grind bars had given him confidence. Casey had also thrown him some useful advice. "Commitment is the key," he said. "I've seen fear hurt a lot of people."

Alex tried to remember the first part and forget the second. He twisted his hips 90 degrees backside so the underside of the deck landed on the rail — and he nailed it — sliding down like there was no tomorrow. Of course if it went wrong there probably wouldn't be a tomorrow (well, not one he'd remember), but if he pulled it off he'd skate right into video history.

A face flashed across his line of vision. At the time he hardly noticed, as he was focused on the ground flying up at him at the speed of a Pentium 20. *Bang!* He landed hard. He bent his knees to absorb the shock, and he almost had it nailed. However, he didn't straighten the board out properly so his balance was skewed, and by trying to hold it as long as possible for the video, he didn't run off when he had the chance. There was only one thing he could do: bail.

For a split second his right arm thought about breaking the fall, but skateboarding instinct took over. Any boarder knows that putting a hand down means six weeks of having kids decorate your cast. Alex took the concrete on his hip and shoulder, did two side rolls and skipped back to his feet. He was hacked that he'd missed the trick, but at least he was getting better at falling onto concrete.

"Don't worry," said Casey, still looking through the camera as Alex limped over. "I can send that one to Funniest Home Videos; probably win a fortune."

"You're funny," said Alex. "Turn that thing off now."

"Not yet. I just want to see your reaction."

"Does it look like I'm chucking a spaz?"

"Not that reaction. This reaction."

Alex wondered what the hell he was talking about.

"Hello Alex," a girl's voice said out of nowhere.

Alex jerked his head around but could see nothing.

"We shared a few good times in the AV room at school. Remember me?"

What is this? This is your life?

Suddenly, a body popped up from behind the embankment. A very good-looking body.

"Thought we'd surprise you," said Casey.

Alex stood there, his mouth catching flies.

"Well, aren't you going to say hi to an old friend?" the girl said.

"Hi Becky," Alex said meekly.

Casey turned the camera off and laughed. "This video is going to win an Academy Award!"

If Casey wasn't such a good mate, Alex would have been tempted to drop his stupid video camera down the vert ramp.

CHAPTER 2

She's Gone

Amazing Italian facts according to Becky Tonella:

- Teenagers zoom around frenetic Italian streets on motorscooters wearing only T-shirts and hair for protection. Becky sneaks on the back of her friend's bike when her mum's not looking.

- They keep the heads of saints in jars.

- People eat dinner at 9.30 pm. Before dinner, instead of watching television everybody strolls around the town square. The young ladies dress in black miniskirts and walk white poodles and the young men yell out "Bella" (beautiful).

- Becky could speak Italian almost fluently, even though she had lived there only eight months.

Becky Tonella's not so amazing Italian facts:

- Becky was going back to Italy. Soon. Today was the only day they would spend together.

Alex was trying hard to be happy. Becky was

back, live in the flesh. Her jet-black hair had grown long, and she wore it out so it fell halfway down her back. Alex touched her, to make sure she was real, and she took his hand and smiled. A beautiful, happy smile, not the sad smile she used to give. She talked much more than Alex remembered, and there were no awkward, fingernail-staring silences between them like there once were. She waved her spare hand around as she gabbed about Italy, her relatives, even her dad. He should be out of jail in six months, she said. But through all of this, a nagging thought was at the back of Alex's mind. Becky was going back to Italy. Soon.

"When are you coming back to live?" he asked over lunch at his house.

"Let's enjoy today," said Becky.

"I am. I just want to know when."

"Don't know. Mum's got a job in Italy now, and Nonna and Nonno said we can stay as long as we like."

"Don't you miss your dad?"

"Of course. I write to him twice a week. But Mum still hasn't forgiven him."

"It's not like he killed anyone."

"Try and tell Mum that."

Becky's dad was a lawyer who had been caught

stealing his clients' money. After he was convicted, Becky moved to Logan City, where she went to school at St Joseph's. Through a combination of trickery and good fortune, Alex managed to go out with her. Not long after, however, she went to live in Italy with her grandparents.

"Hey Becky," said Sam, walking in with her best friend and neighbour, Mandy Lee, "what are Italian guys like?"

"Are they cuter than Beeton guys?" asked Mandy. "It wouldn't be hard."

Becky laughed. "They are cute. You should see them ski down the mountain, legs flexing …"

"That'll do," said Alex.

"But even so," continued Becky giving Alex a dirty look for interrupting, "they're not nearly as cool as some Aussie guys. One especially."

"I find that hard to believe," said Sam.

After lunch Alex and Becky took a bus to the Logan Hyperdome. They both had about 5 bucks and Becky suggested they split up for 15 minutes and buy each other a present.

"Something to remind us of today," Becky said.

Alex thought about buying Becky a miniature skateboard but he ended up getting her a necklace. It was a clear purple stone in the shape of a heart on a sterling silver chain. It actually cost $50, and Alex almost cleaned out his savings account when he withdrew the money from the ATM. When he gave it to Becky she planted a kiss right on his lips and immediately slipped it on.

Becky led Alex to an instant photo booth outside of Kmart. They squeezed in and Becky directed them into different poses and positions. There was only a second or two between photos and in most they looked like stunned rabbits. One, though, of Becky sitting on Alex's lap, smiling at him while he looked into the camera, turned out nice. She put the photo inside the frame she had bought and gave it to Alex, telling him never to forget her. He said he didn't need a photo for that.

Soon it was time to go, and reality hit them along with a blast of hot air as they waited outside for their buses. Becky was going to the city, Alex home to Beeton.

There didn't seem much to say. They would keep emailing, of course. Becky would send over an Italian skateboarding magazine, so Alex could see what tricks they could pull over there. Alex would say hi to Jimmy Homan and Sarah Sceney for her.

"Will you miss me?" said Becky, turning towards him.

"Maybe …"

"Maybe?" she said, putting her arms around Alex's neck. "What sort of answer is that?"

"Maybe I will and maybe I won't."

Becky leant in close, their noses almost touching.

"If you want a kiss you'd better say you'll miss me."

"I'll miss you."

Alex was surprised he remembered how to kiss. It had been a long time since he'd practised, but he had two advantages:

1. He was kissing the same girl as last time — the girl who'd taught him everything he knew about kissing, which wasn't all that much but right now seemed enough.

2. He'd visualised that kiss every night since. A teacher once told him that the brain can't differentiate between imagination and real life, which is why mental imagery is so effective for learning skills such as skateboarding. And kissing.

Mental imagery can be unreliable, however. It depends on what you notice at the time. That night, as Alex tried to replay every moment of the kiss, he realised he didn't notice all that much. He was aware of Becky's hand rubbing circles on his lower back. He remembered her mouth slightly widen as their lips touched. And the next thing he knew she was on the bus. Alex tried to drift back to the kiss, but Becky sitting by the window, waving goodbye, kept playing over and over in his head.

CHAPTER 3
Downer

At the skatepark, when Casey and Alex were ripping it up everyone skated well. If Casey nailed a kickflip on the ramp, then some beginner would land his first ever kickflip on the flat. Good events led to other good events. Unfortunately, it was the same when bad things happened. Becky's leaving sparked a chain reaction of the negative kind.

The Jacksons were robbed. It was right before the school year started while the family was on a day trip to Mt Tamborine. The thief smashed Alex's bedroom window to get in and took everything of value in the house. The only thing Alex had of value was his skateboard, but luckily he'd taken this with him in case he found some concrete in the rainforest. He had his CD player stolen, but it didn't work too well anyway, so getting a new one from the insurance was a bonus. Alex's mum, however, was devastated. Her white diamond bracelet that had been passed down through four generations was gone.

"It's irreplaceable," said Sharon quietly as she buried her head in Chief's huge shoulder.

"I'll ask the guys down the gym to keep their ears to the ground," he replied. "We might be able to track it down. Usually stolen jewellery ends up in pawn shops."

Chief knew about these things. When he was young he hadn't always been on the right side of the law.

"Jeff, this wouldn't happen if we lived in a decent suburb," said Sharon, quickly turning from sad to mad. "There are break-ins every night, drug dealers on street corners. It's time we cut our losses."

Jeff was Chief's real name, though only Sharon used it.

"Let's shift to the beach," said Sam. "I can get a tan and check out the surfers."

"We're not moving anywhere," said Chief. "This place has been good to us. One event doesn't a bad life make."

"Speak much?" said Sam.

Sharon didn't tell Sam to mind her manners like she usually did. She was in her own world, staring out of the broken window.

* * *

After that day things were tense in the Jackson household. You could hear Chief and Sharon talking in muffled voices late at night, which wasn't at all like Chief as he got up at 5 am to work out. Alex couldn't hear much of what they were saying, but one time he heard his mum say something about "growing up in a safe environment", and Chief reply with "we're as safe as houses".

Not the best analogy, Alex thought.

"I bet you five bucks we move by Easter," Sam said to Alex. "What Mum wants, she gets."

"We can't afford to move," Alex replied. "Mum does all right, but Dad gets paid bugger all."

"What do you think they're fighting about, stupid? Mum wants Dad to give up the job at the gym and find a better one."

Chief not training the boys? Alex couldn't believe it. "Don't call me stupid, stupid."

In a few weeks the talking had stopped but the tension remained. Newspapers were left around the house opened at the Employment section. There were brochures from TAFE cluttering up the kitchen bench. One of them described a course that trained you to be a security guard. Alex tried to imagine Chief standing outside a bank with a gun and a uniform. The only uniform Chief ever wore was shorts, singlet, and a tattoo of a crossed pair of boxing gloves on his arm. The only weapon he needed was his fists.

One night over dinner Chief said that he had an announcement to make. Sharon looked interested. He had been made an offer, he said. Sharon looked excited. There was a Queensland Junior Boxing team travelling to Russia and he had been asked to be the coach. They'd be away for five weeks. He wouldn't make much money, but it was an all-expenses-paid trip. One of the boys from his club, Ben Wilson, had been asked to go. He's a real good boy, Chief said. Sharon looked down at her food. She didn't look up for a long time.

CHAPTER 4
Year 9 Is Gay

As soon as Mr Graham had finished explaining the English oral — which was to design your own radio program and present it to the class either live or on a tape — Billy Johnstone had his hand up.

"Are we allowed to use a dictaphone to record the radio program?" he asked.

"Yes Billy, you may."

"So we can use a dictaphone?"

"Yes."

Zane Beard yelled out a question. "Are we being marked on our diction, sir?"

"Of course," said Mr Graham.

"This assignment scares the dickens out of me," Zane continued. "Would you be able to dictate exactly what I have to do?"

Alex sighed. This prank was funny the first five times they pulled it, but it was starting to get old. Small giggles spread around the room.

"It's 3–2 to Beard," Peter Callaghan whispered to Alex and Jimmy.

"I'll tell you what I'll do," said Mr Graham to Zane. "I'll DICtate it to both you and Billy at lunchtime. You can meet me here at 12.45."

It took the boys a few seconds to realise they'd been given a detention. "Awww, what for, sir? I didn't do nuthin'!" Billy said.

"I know you didn't, Billy, but being a DICtator, I insist that you and Zane come back at lunch, where I will perform a DIChotomy on you. Oh, by the way, DIChotomy means to split into two. And make sure you bring your DICtionaries with you, as I want you to look up the word DICtum, and write out its meaning one hundred times."

The class giggled.

"What a dick," Billy mumbled under his breath.

"What's that, Billy? I didn't hear you. Do you have a DICky tongue?" Mr Graham said. "And if I'm not mistaken, I've just won the first set against both of you, 7–6."

Everyone, except Billy Johnstone and Zane Beard, laughed. Alex hadn't been looking forward to English this year, as he was in an all-boys' class. Something to do with helping boys do better at English and letting the girls "express" themselves in a safe (i.e. no boys) environment. But luckily it looked like Mr Graham, who was a new teacher at St Joseph's, could hold his own. He'd need to be able to.

Things had changed since Year 8. Now, more than ever, it was about image. If you drank, smoked, were bad in class, good at footy, and "hooked in" with girls — you were cool. If you were fat, skinny, wore glasses, were real smart or real dumb, played a musical instrument (other than guitar or drums), danced (other than moshing), dressed or looked funny — you got caned. The kids still remembered Alex's fights with Billy Johnstone last year, so no one messed with him. But they didn't think he was cool, either. Mostly, they left him alone.

But other boys in Year 9 got it bad. And it wasn't so much the dead legs, mugby tackles, bag/hat/lunch stealing that seemed to hurt them. It was being called gay. There was nothing worse for a boy in Year 9 than to be labelled a poofter, and no one copped more stick than John Carson-Zanger.

John had frizzy brown hair and wore his socks and pants a bit too high. His family emigrated from Romania less than a year ago, and his English wasn't the best. He tended to get his words mixed up, especially when under stress.

"I will burn youse house down!" he said after Billy flicked him on the side of the head with a pen.

"I will burn youse dresses," replied Billy. "The ones you wear to pick up men at night."

Even with the mixed-up words and the uncool dress sense, it wouldn't have been so bad if John had learnt to keep his mouth shut when he was stirred. But he bit every time. Alex didn't speak much to John. He was glad it wasn't him getting the hard time.

"After this radio program is completed," said Mr Graham, "we can start on a new unit I think many of you will enjoy. It's called 'Skateboarding'."

This class is getting better all the time.

CHAPTER 5
Go Home, Pig!

"As a representative of your local police force, I am very glad to have the opportunity of addressing you today at your school assembly."

"He's probably making a drug bust," whispered Peter Callaghan, sitting on Alex's right.

"We take our responsibility of protecting you and all the citizens of Logan City very seriously. Part of our job is not only to arrest people who are doing the wrong thing, but also to educate and help the youth in our community. Each year we run a special program for juvenile offenders called 'Break the Cycle, not the Law'. The money we receive from your fundraising allows us to keep the program going, and keep more young people out of jail."

"I bet he uses the money to buy his kid's birthday presents," said Peter, talking behind his hand.

Mrs Blake threw a scowl in their direction.

"To show our appreciation of your efforts, the Logan City Police would like to present the principal of St Joseph's College, Mr Stahl, with this outdoor clock."

There was stilted applause as the policeman handed Mr Stahl an expensive-looking clock and shook his hand for the all-important photo — a certain inclusion in the next school newsletter.

Full school assemblies meant 45 minutes of sitting on the concrete, getting shooshed by teachers and watching endless presentations. They were, by definition, boring, but usually something unplanned happened which made them bearable.

"GO HOME, PIG!"

In the undercover area the words bounced violently off the walls. For a few seconds there was dead silence, then muffled laughter by one or two students spread like a Mexican wave at the footy.

"Who was it?" kids murmured. It had been a boy, but that's all anybody could tell. You would have to be very brave, very stupid, or both to try such a thing at assembly. If caught you'd probably get your tongue chopped off.

The whole school was looking up at the Year 10 section. The deputy, Mr Dowden, stepped up to the microphone. "Quiet please, everyone. QUIET!"

Mr Dowden had been deputy of St Joseph's for 16 years, and he was authority in a sweaty shirt and pooh-brown tie. The noise dropped to a low din and then to nothing at all.

"I would ask that at the end of this assembly all Year 10s please stay behind."

They groaned.

"I expect the person who made that unfortunate remark to make themselves known at that time. I apologise to Senior Sergeant Doyle and assure him that this is the sentiment of one attention-seeking individual and not that of the whole school. I ask that we put our hands together again for Sergeant Doyle."

The students, feeling a mixture of guilt and excitement, clapped loudly.

"This should remind us all of the importance of being respectful. Respectful to each other, respectful to ourselves, and respectful to our school property."

School assemblies were also about long lectures from the deputy principal.

"It causes me great sadness to report that the amount of graffiti at this school is much greater than at any other time in our 20-year history. Much of it has been the work of one group, who I won't give the pleasure of naming."

Adrian Dorry, sitting behind, tapped Alex on the shoulder. "It's SWA," he whispered. "It's written over half the books in the library."

Mrs Blake was staring again.

"The act of vandalism is a low, selfish thing to be involved in," Mr Dowden continued. "It costs us a great deal of time and money to clean up so you can have a school you're proud to attend. It is NOT ON. I can't be any clearer than that. I would ask that anyone who has any information on this group contact me immediately. It is not dobbing your friends in, it is showing that you care about your school and its property."

Adrian leant forward. "I heard SWA's against authority and stuff. It was probably one of them who yelled out."

"What's SWA mean?" asked Alex. He didn't look at Adrian but forward at the stage. He could sense Mrs Blake was ready to make a bust.

"Don't know," he said. "But I know who's in it. Some Year 10 guys and a chick."

There were more presentations happening. The art teacher was gushing into the microphone.

"The winner is one of the most talented painters St Joseph's has had in a long time. From Year 10, Kimberley Lim."

Alex couldn't see the girl properly as the policeman was blocking his view. The name was familiar, though, and he had almost placed her when he was distracted. She received, along with a certificate, a loud wolf-whistle — again from the Year 10 section.

Adrian tapped him on the shoulder.

"That's ..." was all Adrian got the chance to say. He did, however, get the chance to share his lunchtime with Mrs Blake.

CHAPTER 6
Girl Problems

Jimmy was having girl problems. He and Sarah Sceney had been going out for eight months, but things were rocky. In primary school Sarah was known for two things: embarrassing the boy she had had a crush on for five years — which was Alex — and getting A's in every subject.

In high school she kept getting A's but stopped liking Alex. She got together with Jimmy and they were a good match, with their pet names for each other and the way they exchanged emails every day, even though they only lived a five-minute walk from each other's houses.

But over the Christmas holidays Sarah's parents split up. Her dad, who gave her $5 for every A on her report card, took off to Sydney with a younger woman. Sarah took it out on her mum — an older-looking version of Sarah, glasses and all.

"If you didn't nag him all the time this never would have happened," Sarah said.

"I did the best I could," said Mrs Sceney. "I wish he could say the same."

All the money Sarah saved from her A's was spent on changing her looks. She swapped her glasses for contact lenses and bought a whole new wardrobe. Both Jimmy and Alex thought this strange. You'd expect Sarah Sceney to buy the new Encyclopedia Britannica CD, not a halter-top from JeansWest.

Jimmy also took some heat. Sarah accused him of not finding her attractive and looking at other girls. The only girl Jimmy looked at was Lara Croft on his Sony PlayStation. She said Jimmy didn't like her anymore, even though he bought her a 12-month subscription to *Science and Nature Online Magazine* for Christmas. She said Jimmy was more interested in his computer than her. Well, she had a point there.

"What should I do, mate?" Jimmy asked Alex as they lined up to buy some Redskins at the canteen. "I feel like I don't know who me girlfriend is anymore."

Alex was about to say something, then remembered that it wasn't long ago that he'd been asking Jimmy's advice about Becky. Jimmy's advice caused him to lie and get beaten up by Billy Johnstone. He decided to think for a few more seconds.

"Emma Barney is having a party next Friday and Sarah wants to go," Jimmy continued. "She's even bought a new dress. Do you reckon I should go with her?"

Out of the corner of his eye Alex could see Sarah standing outside of Block 1. She was talking to, of all people, Billy Johnstone.

"I reckon you should."

"Well, if I'm going you're coming too. I hate those things. Too much pressure."

* * *

That afternoon Alex hung out at Casey's place. At 19 Casey was the idol of Beeton skate-groms, pulling moves that most kids only dream about. He lived in a one-bedroom flat squashed against the train line. It was loud but Casey didn't mind. The punk music he listened to was usually louder.

They had a look at their skateboarding video, which a mate of Casey's had edited together. It was impressive for a production with a budget of $30 (a video tape and a couple of pizzas for the editor) — with slow motion, fades, fast music and lots of sick tricks.

Alex's boardslide down the rail had got a guernsey, slam and all.

"I would have cut it right when I landed," Alex said.

"I told him to leave it in," said Casey. "People like to have a laugh."

"Watch this," Casey said as Becky appeared on the video screen popping up from behind the embankment.

They cracked up at the gobsmacked look on Alex's face. Casey had zoomed in for a close-up.

"You barstool," Alex said. Though he had to admit it was good to see Becky again. Even if it was only on video.

Inspired by their first film-making experience they cruised to the skatepark. Alex pulled a few k-grinds and boardslides on the grind bar. He was getting his confidence back, though he wasn't game to take on the rail. Maybe next video.

Casey hit the vert and nailed a sweet Japan Air. He was doing scary stuff lately — he'd even landed a 540 rocket grab. No wonder he was sponsored by SkateBiz.

After a while they took a breather, raiding the esky in the boot of Casey's rustbucket of a car. "I'm gonna miss this place," said Casey, "especially that mother of a thing." He looked up at the 2-metre vert ramp he had practically grown up on.

"You going to the coast or something?" Alex asked.

"Nah. Europe."

"Europe! When? Why? How long?"

Casey smiled. "I leave next week. I'll be gone a few months, I s'pose. It depends. Why do you reckon I'm going?"

"To skate?"

"Nah, to ski."

They chuckled.

Bad luck is supposed to happen in threes, Alex thought. First Becky leaving, then the house getting robbed, and now Casey taking off to Europe.

Bad luck for some is good luck for others. It was Casey's dream to hit the pro skateboarding tour. Now he was living it.

"Show the world how to skate, mate," Alex said, shaking his hand.

"I'll try," Casey said.

"Don't try. Do it."

CHAPTER 7
Sicko Analysis

"Is anyone in this class a good skateboarder?" asked Mr Graham.

It was week 5 and the radio unit had been and gone. Alex and Jimmy had scored a B+ for their radio program — with Jimmy using his wide range of women's voices and Alex playing the straight man.

"I rock!" answered Zane Beard. "Yesterday I landed a nollie heelflip down four stairs."

"You did not," said Billy Johnstone. "You can't even ollie."

Alex was surprised that Billy Johnstone knew what an ollie was.

Jimmy put his hand up. "Alex is one of the best skateboarders in the school. Last year he organised a skateboarding demonstration and he fifty-fiftied down the library stairs."

"Those big stairs?" asked Mr Graham.

"Yep."

"Sounds dangerous."

"It was right after Billy threw his head into a steel post and his girlfriend ran away," said Peter Callaghan. "He wasn't thinking straight."

The class laughed. Alex gave Peter a dirty look.

"Well Alex, you should be a big help during this unit. Through reading, watching, and talking about skateboarding, we hope to understand what makes a skateboarder tick."

Just what I need. A bit of sicko analysis.

Mr Graham handed out an article from a skateboarding magazine for the class to read. It was about boarders being picked up by the police for riding in places where they weren't allowed. It didn't recommend against skating in these places, but instead told you what to do if the police nabbed you. Always have a fake name and address handy, it said.

Mr Graham asked what this showed about how skateboarders were portrayed by the media.

"They're telling the truth," said Peter Callaghan. "Skateboarders are nut cases."

"What do you think, Alex?" asked Mr Graham.

"It's showing how skateboarders are picked on,"

he said. "Most boarders don't want to hurt anybody. They just want to skate."

"Then why don't they use skateparks instead of public property?"

Good question.

"They're trying to show that they can skate anywhere they want," said Jimmy. "If it's illegal it's more fun."

"Exactly," said Mr Graham. "Often these magazines show skateboarders as frustrated and rebelling against society. I want to find out whether or not this is true."

"I want to know where Carson-Zanger lives," said Zane Beard, "so I can give his name and address to the cops when I get picked up."

"You just want to go to his house tonight," said Billy Johnstone. "So you can get lucky."

"I will burn both youse houses down!" John said loudly.

Mr Graham wrote Billy and Zane's names on the board. It looked like they had another detention.

"Our major piece of assessment will be a small-group presentation on the attitude of skateboarders compared with the way they are portrayed by the media," Mr Graham said. "You will need to interview a local skateboarder as well as show and discuss some video footage. I would like you to get into groups of two or three."

"Guaranteed A, mate," said Jimmy, turning to Alex.

Everyone quickly found a group, except for John Carson-Zanger, who was left on his own. "You can join in with Alex and Jimmy," said Mr Graham.

Jimmy and Alex looked at each other but didn't say anything. John was giving them his best crooked-tooth smile.

CHAPTER 8
No Frills

The rest of the week in English they studied skatey videos and magazines, which didn't seem like study to Alex. Mr Graham pointed out that the pro boarders rarely wore helmets or pads, and asked the class why they thought this was the case.

"They're nut cases," said Peter Callaghan.

Mr Graham asked Alex if he wore protective equipment.

"I wear a helmet and pads when I'm skating the vert," he said. "But otherwise I don't wear anything. It's just not … done."

"Alex doesn't need protection," said Zane Beard. "His girlfriend lives in Italy."

"He doesn't have a girlfriend," said Billy Johnstone. "He goes out with John Carson-Zanger."

Zane laughed loudly.

John stood up and looked like he was going to

take a swing at Billy, but Mr Graham got between them.

This time there was no detention for Billy and Zane. They got to visit the Year 9 coordinator instead.

Working with John Carson-Zanger wasn't as bad as Alex expected. John knew almost nothing about skateboarding but he knew a lot about hip-hop, which was Alex's favourite type of music. John said hip-hop was big in Romania, and he even lent Alex some of his CDs.

John also knew a fair bit about computers, and he agreed with one of Jimmy's theories — that Apple Macs were better than IBMs. Both of John's parents were computer engineers, which is how they got a visa to migrate to Australia. They didn't have good jobs yet, he said. They were having a hard time with their English.

It took their group about two minutes to work out that Jimmy and John would use their computer skills to put the presentation onto Power-Point, Alex would be the skateboarder they would analyse, and Casey's video would be their discussion tool. "Just as long as we don't show my slam," Alex said. For the rest of the allocated assignment time they debated whether Eminem or Ice-T was the better rapper. Alex liked the classic hip-hop, John the angrier, modern stuff.

"Eminem, he bad," said John.

"Ice-T is cool," said Alex.

"You guys are sad," said Jimmy.

Another distraction from work was Emma Barney's party, which according to Adrian Dorry almost the whole of Year 9 was attending, plus a heap of Year 10s. "The rule is that everybody puts in five bucks, and Emma's older brother is going to supply the grog," said Adrian. "He might even get a few joints."

"If we get the girls real drunk, you never know what will happen," said Peter Callaghan.

"They might puke in your lap, Callaghan," said Jimmy.

*　*　*

"Are we sponsored by no-frills, Mum?" asked Alex that night. Around the house there were no-frills cereal, no-frills dishwashing liquid and even no-frills toilet paper.

"We're not sponsored by anybody," she replied, looking up from the kitchen bench where she was helping Sam with her maths homework. "You have to pay for everything in life."

As well as tightening up her already frugal

spending habits, Alex's mum was working over-time. She was saving money for something and it certainly wasn't for Chief to have a good time in Russia.

"Hey Shaz, have you seen my black singlet?" asked Chief. He was running late for his nightly training session with the boys.

"I threw it out," she said. "It stunk."

"But it was my favourite singlet," Chief pro-tested. "Why didn't you just wash it?"

She shrugged, and went back to explaining frac-tions.

Alex had never seen his mum act like this before. Now he knew what other kids were talking about when they said their parents didn't get along. He decided that he, the eldest child, had better do something.

"Mum, are you mad because Chief doesn't earn enough money as a boxing trainer for us to move out of Beeton?"

"Mmm," she said, not looking up.

"And Chief, are you upset because Mum doesn't respect what you do, and because you think Bee-ton is the bees knees and Mum doesn't like it?"

Chief grunted.

"Well, I think I've got an answer," Alex said.

Everybody looked at him now, even Sam.

"I could quit school, go on the pro skateboarding tour with Casey Marshall and earn enough money for us all to move to that new estate in Logan City. Then Chief could keep his job, Mum would be happy and we'd all live happily ever after."

Chief went to find another singlet and Sharon looked down at a textbook called 'Future Maths 7'.

"You're an idiot," said Sam.

"I could do it. I'm sponsored, you know!" said Alex.

"You are not. Casey Marshall got you a board from his sponsor."

"Shut up."

Later that night Alex heard Chief and his mum talking in muffled voices. He heard footsteps down the hall and saw his dad's silhouette in the bedroom doorway.

"You awake, son?" said Chief.

"I am now."

"You know …" He paused, searching for the right words. "Just because your mum and me aren't seeing eye to eye at the moment, well, that doesn't mean you have to worry."

"Why do you have to go to Russia, Dad?"

"Cause it's something I want to do, have to do. I dunno."

"Why does Mum want to get out of Beeton so bad?"

"You'll have to ask her. There is a bit of riff-raff around, though, I'll admit that."

"Good night, Chief."

"Night champ."

"Hey Chief."

"What?"

"Will you ask Mum if I can go to a party tomorrow night?"

"I'll see what I can do."

A few minutes later Sam crept in. "Can't a bloke get some shut-eye around here?" Alex said.

"Do you think they'll get a divorce?" asked Sam.

"Mum and Dad? No way."

"I hope not." She paused. "If they do get a divorce, do you think I'll live with Mum and you'll live with Chief?"

"They're not getting a divorce. They're safe as hou … I mean a bank."

"Because even though you're stupid sometimes, I don't want us to live apart."

"Yeah, then you wouldn't know all my secrets," he said, smiling.

Even though it was dark, he knew that Sam was smiling too.

CHAPTER 9
The Party

"I don't have a good feeling about this," said Sharon as she dropped Alex and Jimmy off at Emma Barney's house.

There were kids hanging around outside, smoking, and in the Corona you could no longer hear the 60s music of Sharon's favourite radio station over the thumping bass coming from inside the house.

Boom, boom, boom.

"Perhaps I should go in and meet the girl's parents," said Sharon.

"We'll be right, Mum," Alex said quickly. "You can trust us, can't she Jimmy?"

"You can trust us, Mrs J. We're Catholic school-boys, remember?"

"That's what I'm afraid of. Well, I'm picking you boys up at 11. If there's any trouble, call me straightaway, Alex."

"No worries, Mum."

Alex was glad his mum didn't come inside to meet Emma Barney's parents. Not only because of the embarrassment factor but because her parents were away for the weekend. They had left Emma's 18-year-old brother, Jordie, in charge of the house. Jordie was sucking on a beer with his arm around a Year 9 girl, Claire Carney.

Good move, Mr and Mrs Barney.

They went in and saw Sarah across the other side of the room. Her new dress was short and silky and her black hair done up in frizzes and curls. She had on bright red lipstick and a little too much make-up, but even Alex had to admit she looked good. For a nerd.

"You're a lucky bloke," he said to Jimmy.

They went over and chatted, though it was impossible to hear much. Jimmy yelled three times to Sarah that she looked good. When she finally heard him she smiled but didn't return the compliment. Jimmy was wearing cargo pants and thongs. Emma came over offering drinks, and Sarah asked for a wine cooler.

"Want a beer?" Emma said to Alex.

"Maybe later," he said.

Emma looked at Jimmy.

"Yeah, later for me too."

"You guys are hopeless," said Sarah. She walked away.

Jimmy looked hurt.

"She's probably just gone to the toilet," Alex yelled in his ear.

A few seconds later Jimmy punched Alex's arm. "Look," he said, pointing towards the doorway. John Carson-Zanger had walked in. He was scanning the room trying to find a non-hostile face and gave a toothy grin when he spotted Alex and Jimmy.

Before he made it across the crowded room he ran into Billy Johnstone. Literally. Billy's beer went all over Zane Beard's new Rip Curl shirt.

Billy turned to see who the culprit was. Alex gave Jimmy a nudge and they hurried over. John would have a short and not very memorable party if Billy got hold of him.

Alex felt a tightening in the pit of his stomach. Last year he fought Billy twice, and if you were a boxing commentator you'd say they shared the honours. Billy received some nasty cuts and bruises, and Alex had to go to the hospital with concussion. Well, maybe Billy won on points.

Alex and Jimmy grabbed an arm each and

whisked John out of the room. Behind him Alex could hear Billy yelling but he didn't turn around to find out what he was saying.

They opened a door at the end of the hallway.

"I think we should stay here for a while," Alex said.

Jimmy nodded. "Why'd you come here?" he asked John.

John shrugged. "It's a party, hey? You know, dance, meet girls."

"Get bashed," added Jimmy.

John shrugged. "Look," he said. There was a computer in the corner.

"It's an Apple," said Jimmy. "I wonder if there's any good games?" He switched it on.

"What are you going to do about your girlfriend?" asked Alex.

"I'd better go tell her where I am," said Jimmy with a sigh. "You stay here with John."

"Nah, I'll go tell her. You guys play games," said Alex. He wasn't into computers much.

"Stay away from Johnstone," Jimmy warned.

The party was in full swing. Zane Beard was dancing topless on the table, swinging his beer-soaked shirt above his head. The music was cranked up so loud the room was vibrating, and newly formed couples had drifted to spare couches or corners — playing tonsil hockey. Alex looked over to see Jordie on the couch with Claire Carney, his tongue working its way down her throat. Claire was a nice girl but she had a reputation to live up to. Her nickname was CC, not only because of her initials but because of the slogan "she can't say no".

"Have you seen Sarah?" Alex asked Emma.

"I think she's out the back."

Outside Alex tripped over a huge potplant that had been tipped over. There was smashed glass on the patio, and the well-kept yard was strewn with bottles and cigarette butts. Even so, Alex liked it better out here. It wasn't so loud that you couldn't think and there was a breeze that whisked away some of the stench of spilt beer.

Someone tapped him on the shoulder. "You're Alex, aren't you?"

He turned around. It was a girl who looked familiar.

"I'm Kim," she said.

Alex nodded. *Of course. Kimberley Lim.* She was one of the skaters in last year's demonstration at school, pulling some sweet 50–50s and noseslides on the kerb.

She was wearing 3/4 length pants, a black SMP

T-shirt and a pair of Osiris shoes. Those skate shoes weren't cheap. Alex usually wore his trusty Dunlop Volleys for skating, which weren't the greatest when it came to cushioning but had good grip.

"I saw you at assembly," he said. "You won that art comp."

"They made me go up the front. It was embarrassing."

"You still skate?"

"Skated here. You?"

"Not here. But I still skate."

"Come meet the guys," she said. "We skate around Beeton every Friday night."

He followed her over to a group of four boys sitting on the grass. Alex recognised a few of them from school. They were in Year 10 and seemed friendly enough, even though they were smoking and drinking beer.

"Remember the grommet last year who grinded the library rail? Well this is him — Alex," said Kim. "This is Steve, Nugget, Cookie and Goof."

"G'day," said everybody.

"Aren't you mates with Casey Marshall?" said Steve.

"Yeah."

"He used to be best mates with my brother

Ryan. They used to rip Beeton apart in their younger days."

Alex had never heard Casey mention him. "Casey's in Europe now," said Alex. "Skating pro."

"My brother said he was the best skater he'd ever seen. Other than him."

They talked for a while — about equipment, tricks, good places to rip. Alex had never seen them at the skatepark. "Why didn't you go in the demo last year?" he asked.

"That stuff's for show," said Steve. "That same afternoon, after school, I came back and board-slided the library stairs."

Kim must have noticed that Alex looked doubtful.

"I was there," said Kim. "Steve's an awesome skater. Best in the school."

Alex might have had something to say about that. Then he remembered there were four Year 10 boys in front of him, and a Year 9 boy nearby who'd love to see him bashed. He let it slide.

"Why don't you come down to the skatebowl tomorrow?" Alex asked.

"We don't skate in parks," Steve said. "Only street."

"You should come skating with us," said Kim.

"Maybe," said Alex. He knew there were two chances his mum would let him skate in downtown Beeton on a Friday night.

"We should cruise," said Steve, taking one last puff on his smoke before flicking it onto the lawn. "Watch this," he said to Alex.

He grabbed his board and took off down the patio, heading straight for a couple lying on the ground. Right before he smacked into their heads he popped a fat ollie over the top of them and landed smooth.

The guy can skate.

"Catchya Alex," said Kim.

Alex took another look at the couple on the patio. They hadn't even twigged that they had just been used as a high-jump bar, their entangled mouths not coming up for air. Alex remembered that he was supposed to be looking for Sarah, then realised he was looking right at her. She was on the patio, kissing Billy Johnstone.

CHAPTER 10
Becky

To: **alexjackson@skunkmail.com.au**
From: **Beckyt13@hotmail.com**

Dearest Alex,

Buongiorno! Sorry it's been a few weeks since I wrote, but I've been settling back into Italian life. Everything is so slow here, I think it is rubbing off on me. It's freezing, but the good thing about the weather is I get to go skiing! I went with a friend whose family owns a chateau in the Swiss Alps. It was beautiful and lots of fun. You should try it some time, though knowing you you'd be a crazy snowboarder.

Guess what? I got a call from Casey. He's in Germany at the moment getting ready for a competition. In a few weeks he's coming to Trieste and I've asked Mum if we can go and watch him skate. I hope she lets me. He said to say hi, and that he'll call you when he wins some money.

How is Year 9? Is it heaps different from Year 8? School over here is pretty easy. We start at 7 in the morning and finish by 1. Then we go home and sleep.

I'm really happy I saw you last month. I miss you heaps and I still wear the necklace you bought for me. It's hard being away from you, especially when I'm not sure how long we'll be apart. Do you think we'll last? Long-distance relationships suck.

I keep thinking about you and look forward to the day we can be together again. I'll try and write more.

Love 4 eva,

Becky.

From: **alexjackson@skunkmail.com.au**
To: **Beckyt13@hotmail.com**

Dear Becky,

Thanks for writing. I was starting to get worried you'd disappeared. It was cool you spoke to Casey. Make sure you go to Trieste (where is that?) and watch him skate. I reckon he'll rip once he gets the hang of the pros.

Things here aren't great. My parents are still not talking and something weird happened last night. There was a party at Emma Barney's house and

Sarah Sceney got with Billy Johnstone.
Jimmy was there but he didn't see. I
can't believe Sarah did that to him.
I know she's your friend, but what a
@#$%!

I'm not sure if I should tell Jimmy.
I want to talk to Sarah and find out
why she did it. I'll let you know how
it turns out.

Of course I think we'll last. As long
as you want us to, that is. I agree
that long-distance relationships suck,
but I'd rather wait for you than go out
with someone I don't like. You have to
talk your mum into moving back to
Australia!
Love,
Alex.
PS. I really liked seeing you too.
PPS. Notice that I am writing back
straightaway.

Alex logged off and waited for Anne, the librarian, to come to the front counter. Last year he and Anne weren't on the best of terms, but lately they'd been getting on like Alex was a regular library nerd. Which, come to think of it, he was. He came in at least once a week to email Becky.

She returned his skateboard. "I was meaning to ask you," she said, "have you seen Sarah lately?"

"Yeah," said Alex.

"She used to come in here almost every day, especially when school started. Do you know what's happened to her?"

"Oh, you know. Probably going through a rebellious stage."

"Sarah as a rebel? That's hard to imagine."

"Were you ever a rebel, Anne?"

She looked startled. "Come to think of it, I suppose I was. A long time ago. Say hello for me, will you. Rebel or not, she's a nice kid."

CHAPTER 11
Gossip and Lies

Alex knocked on the Sceney's front door and waited. He had never been to Sarah's house before. In primary school he'd spent most of his time trying to avoid her, but with the phone calls, notes, letters, poems, rehearsed and impromptu speeches, screensaver messages and compositions — all about him, all about love — it wasn't easy. It was strange that they only became friends once she started going out with Jimmy. But Anne was right — she was a nice girl. Till last night.

No one answered, and Alex breathed a sigh of relief as he made his way down the stairs. Then he heard the door open. He turned to see a dishevelled-looking girl squinting down at him. He looked twice before he realised it was Sarah.

"Alex." She sounded surprised.

"Hi Sarah."

"What are you doing here?"

"I wanted to talk to you about … things."

They went inside. She was still in her Winnie the Pooh pyjamas even though it was almost lunchtime.

"Hard night?" said Alex.

She nodded.

"Where's your mum?" asked Alex.

"Don't know. She left a note but I haven't read it."

Alex wondered how to begin. He decided for the direct approach. "I saw you kissing Billy last night. Billy Johnstone."

She blinked, but otherwise her expression didn't change. If Alex had expected her to break down in tears of guilt, he would have been disappointed.

"Is that what you've come to tell me?"

"Well … yeah. And to find out what you're going to do about Jimmy."

"Does Jimmy know?"

"Not yet."

She was quiet for a few moments and Alex could see her mind ticking over. "Don't tell him anything," she said.

"I was thinking you'd do it for me."

She was quiet again.

"Sarah? You'd better tell him."

"Why?"

"Because …"

"That's a good reason."

"Because if you don't, I will."

She looked at him and her expression changed. Alex had only seen her mad once before and it wasn't the best experience of his life.

"Everyone makes mistakes, you know," she said.

"You cheated on your boyfriend. My best mate. Either you tell him or I will."

"You're so gay."

"What?"

"You heard me. You're a poof."

Alex's right hand made a fist without him realising it. No one said that to Alex Jackson, skateboarder and slayer of the female species. "You had a crush on me for five years, what does that make you?"

She ignored him. "You think you're good but you're not. You're a homo."

"You're a two-timing tart."

Her face instantly tensed and for a second Alex thought she was going to cry. "I'd worry about your own girlfriend if I were you," she said quietly.

"What?"

"Why don't you ask her if she likes Italian boys? Especially rich skiers named Roberto."

"You're a liar."

"You ask her if she went skiing with Roberto at his chateau in Switzerland. Or if she rides on the back of his motorbike. I have email too, you know. Maybe she tells me what she doesn't want you to know?"

Alex wanted to swear at her, hit her, even. But he didn't. He got up and walked out.

"You don't like it, do you?" she said to his back. "Well, Jimmy won't like it either so don't tell him. He doesn't need to know."

Alex had been taught that it was polite to shut the door on your way out. He made sure he was very, very, very polite.

CHAPTER 12
Weeds

Alex thought about going straight to Jimmy's place but he needed time to think. He hung out at the railway station and did some boarding — grinding and sliding along the metal seats.

Becky and an Italian skier? There's no possible way.

But how did Sarah know about Becky's skiing trip, and about her riding on the back of a motor-bike? When Becky told Alex she had done these things with a friend, he naturally thought she meant a girlfriend. But friend could mean boy or girl, couldn't it?

He weighed up the evidence. On the one hand, Becky had always been honest. On the other, people always said that you can't trust anyone — and even *he* had lied to Becky last year. Sarah would have wanted to hurt him after he called her a two-timing tart. Then again, Sarah and Becky were friends, so maybe Becky did tell her things she wouldn't tell Alex.

A voice broke his train of thought. "I thought you only skated where it is legal."

It was Kim. "Sometimes I come here, " he said. "It's not like I can do any more damage to these seats."

"How was the party?" she said.

"Pretty average. Steve's ollie was the highlight of the night."

"He's crazy, that guy. Just like his brother."

"Lots of skaters are."

"Are you?" she asked.

"I try not to be. But it comes naturally."

Kim jumped on her board and tic-tacked till she had enough speed, then ollied up onto the long seat. She slid on the nose for 30 centimetres before she dropped off and landed sketchy.

Alex had a go. He'd practised noseslides at the skatebowl heaps of times, and he slid almost the entire length of the seat before popping off and landing smooth.

"You want me to tell you you're good," she said.

"You don't have to tell me."

"One minute you're running yourself down and the next you're cocky."

"I told you, skateboarders are crazy."

They skated for a long time. Kim took a few falls but jumped right back on. Alex nailed some good boardslides but he still had Becky lingering in the back of his mind. He thought that while he had a female here he should try and get some advice.

"Hey Kim, do you think long-distance relationships can work?"

"Why are you asking me?"

"Well, because you're a girl, and I want to know how girls think."

"Not all girls are the same."

"Yeah, I know. But tell me anyway."

"I don't think any relationships work."

That is different.

"My parents are divorced. Steve's too. I think commitment stuffs things up," she said. "People are meant to be free."

"That's not what I want to hear."

"Your girlfriend's in Italy, isn't she?"

"How do you know?"

"I saw you with her last year. I knew who you were before the skateboarding demonstration. You had a reputation around Beeton as a skate-grom."

Alex liked the sound of that.

"Are you and your girlfriend having trouble?" she asked.

"Maybe. I'm not sure."

He looked at his watch. His mum would be getting worried. "I'd better take off," he said. "Thanks for the skate."

"Come skating with us Friday night."

Alex noticed her smile. It was different from Becky's, but nice. "I'll think about it."

* * *

"The kid's finally home," Chief said as he walked in.

"How'd Ben go?" Alex asked. Chief had been at a boxing tournament most of the day.

"He won in 2. TKO. I tell you that kid will be World Champ one day."

"He has to beat the Russians first."

"You'd better go see your mother," Chief said. "She's not happy with you. We have phones here in Beeton, you know."

"Yeah, sorry. Where is she?"

"Out the back."

Alex passed Sam who was doing Mandy's hair. Dresses were laid out on the bed.

"Where're you two going?" he asked.

"Megan Bell's party," said Sam.

"Will boys be there?"

"Of course!"

"Ooohhh. Boys."

"Shut up."

His mum was in the backyard gardening. She was on her hands and knees attacking weeds with a blunt knife.

"They'd die quicker if you had a real knife," he said.

"I'd be tempted to use it on something other than weeds." She stood up. "You said you'd be gone for an hour and you've been out all day. You didn't even come home for lunch."

"I wasn't hungry."

"Where were you?"

"Around."

"Try again."

Alex sighed. "Library, Sarah Sceney's place and skateboarding. Mostly skateboarding."

"What did you do that was wrong?"

"I forgot to call."

"That's right. I don't want you gallivanting around Beeton all day without knowing where you are. It's not safe."

"Beeton is not that bad."

She ignored him. "What were you doing at Sarah Sceney's house?"

"Talking."

"You're a waterfall of information, aren't you?"

Alex started rocking from one foot to another. His mum always seemed to know when he had a problem and she usually gave good advice. *Dr Mum*, Alex called her. However, he didn't feel in the mood to tell her that his girlfriend might be cheating on him with an Italian skier named Roberto. He didn't feel like telling anybody.

"Sarah's all screwed up since her dad left," he said. "She and Jimmy might be breaking up."

"That's a shame."

Alex looked at his mum's knife. It was black from the dirt. "Why do couples always split up?" he asked.

This caught Sharon off guard, but only for a second. Her two specialties were making banana cake and answering life's tough questions. "Not all couples split up."

"A lot of them do. What goes wrong?"

She looked down. "Relationships are like this garden. It used to be so beautiful. Lots of flowers and no weeds. But underneath the weeds are there, waiting for a chance to grow. If you don't spend time pulling them out they take over."

"Why don't people just pull them out?"

"Too busy. Or sometimes it's too hard."

"What about when they find someone else? Like Mr Sceney?"

"They see a new garden that already has beautiful flowers and no weeds. But maybe they forget that every garden has weeds below the surface, waiting."

Alex looked at his mum's garden and could see what she was talking about. It was a mess after the storms they'd had during the summer. "What are you going to do with this garden?" he said.

"I want to get rid of the weeds," his mum said softly. "I really do. But it's not easy. Sometimes I'd love a bit of help."

"Have you ever asked Chief to help you?"

"Chief? In the garden pulling out weeds? I don't think so."

Alex bent down and grabbed a weed, pulling hard at its roots. It was stubborn but eventually gave way. He helped his mum for 20 minutes, and pulling out one weed at a time they cleared about a third of the back garden. He went inside for a drink.

Sam and Mandy were almost ready.

"Oohh, boys," Alex said, waving his dirty hands close to their sparkling dresses.

"Get lost!"

Chief was watching a video of Ben's fight. "Look at his footspeed," he said excitedly as Alex walked in. "I've never seen a bloke so quick."

"Chief," said Alex. "You ever pulled out weeds before?"

"What?"

"Weeds. In the backyard. You ever helped Mum pull them out?"

"Don't think so."

"Well I reckon you should. It's good training."

"What for? Your legs, when you squat down?"

"Nah. Your marriage."

Chief gave him a funny look. "You're not on drugs, are you champ?"

CHAPTER 13
Turning Rebel

"Skateboarding is a way of life," said Mr Graham. "That's what the magazines and videos tell us. But what sort of life are they promoting? One with crime, drugs and risk taking? Is this what most skateboarders are really like? This is what you will be answering in your presentation next week. Get to work."

Next week? We'd better hurry up.

Alex looked over at Jimmy. He hadn't talked to him since Friday night and it was time to find out how much he knew. "You talked to Sarah lately?" Alex said.

"She rang me Saturday," said Jimmy. "She said she went home from Emma's party early because she wasn't feeling well. That's why you couldn't find her."

He doesn't know much.

John came over. "Hey dudes, what's up?" He'd

learnt most of his English watching American television.

Mr Graham was right behind him. "How are you guys going with your assignment?"

"We're right on schedule," Jimmy said. "Our video is ready to go, and our talk is on PowerPoint on my computer at home."

"Do you have anything I can look at?"

"Umm, not today, sir. I've been having trouble with the printer. Don't worry, we'll be ready to go on the day."

"Mmmm. I hope so. Remember, if you are late it's an automatic fail. I expect something special from you boys — especially with a champion skateboarder in your group."

"That's right, sir. Action Jackson won't let you down," said Jimmy.

Mr Graham went to check on another group. "Jimmy, we haven't even started!" said Alex.

"I'm just telling him what he wants to hear," said Jimmy. "The truth is overrated."

John started rapping, tapping his pencil on the desk to keep the beat. "The truth can cut you deep, when you wake and when you sleep. I only tell my girl what I want for her to keep."

Alex ignored him. "Does Sarah ever talk to you about Becky?" he asked Jimmy.

"Not really. She says they email each other once a week. Why?"

"No reason."

John started rapping again. "A reason, a season, it all adds up to treason …"

The rap was cut short when Billy Johnstone walked past and swiped the pencil out of John's hand. Billy snapped it in two and threw the pieces at John.

"That's for spilling my beer," Billy said.

"Arsehole," whispered Jimmy to his back.

"What's that, Homan?" Billy turned around.

"He called you an arsey hole," John said to Billy.

There is a fine line between guts and stupidity, and John had casually jumped over onto the wrong side.

Billy looked at Jimmy. "Now that your girl-friend's tasted a real man, Homan, I doubt you'll get any girl action for a while. No wonder you and John are best buddies."

"What?" said Jimmy.

"You haven't heard, have you?" said Billy, smil-ing. He gestured towards John and Alex. "You stick

close to your boys. Coz after me she won't settle for what you got."

A few kids sniggered. Alex wasn't one of them. He stood up, seriously invading Billy's personal space. "I think you'd better shut up, Johnstone."

"Who's gonna make me? Yo' mama?"

"Nah, me and my eight friends." Alex clenched his fists.

They eyed off, waiting for the other to throw a punch. Johnstone versus Jackson III was only a nervous twitch away. The fact that they were standing in the middle of a classroom didn't seem to make a scrap of difference.

"Billy, sit down!" ordered Mr Graham from across the room.

He didn't move.

"Billy, NOW!"

Slowly Billy swaggered away, his shoulders pulled back and his cereal-box chest puffed up. "Sarah's tasted a real man now, Homan. There's no going back."

Jimmy's face went a light shade of grey.

"Jimmy, come with me tonight. We burn down his house!" said John.

"You knew about this, didn't you?" Jimmy said to Alex.

Alex looked down. This was going to be a long week.

* * *

At lunchtime Alex filled Jimmy in on what he saw at the party and his visit to Sarah's place. Jimmy said he wanted to be alone for a while. He couldn't believe that Alex hadn't told him straightaway. "I thought we were best mates?" he said.

"We are."

"Best mates tell each other important stuff. How would you like it if I knew something about Becky and didn't tell you?"

"Do you?"

"What?"

"Know something about Becky?"

"No. If I did I'd tell you. That's my point."

Jimmy headed towards the Graphics block and Alex made his way to the library. On his way he saw Kim and the guys sitting at one of the picnic tables outside of Block 4. She called him over.

"How do you get along with Yatesy?" she asked.

Mr Yates was the school librarian. As far as Alex knew he had no overdue library books, so there was no reason to think that his and Mr Yates' relationship was anything but civil.

"Okay, I s'pose."

"Good. We were wondering if you'd do us a favour. We want to watch this skateboarding video in the AV room but we're banned from the library."

"Why?"

"They reckon we've been writing on the books. Even though there's no proof they've still banned us. Typical of this school."

"What do you want me to do?"

"You book an AV room and we'll sneak in through the window."

Alex scratched his head. "I don't think it's a good idea …"

"It's a sick video. You should see the tricks they do. You'll love it."

"Yeah but …"

"If we get caught we'll take the blame. We'll say we forced our way in and there was nothing you could do. Don't worry."

"Live life on the edge," said Steve. "You a skate-boarder or what?"

Alex knew he was succumbing to peer pressure, but he thought, what the heck. What else was he going to do this lunchtime? He went into the library and asked Mr Yates if he could use one of the AV rooms.

"What sort of video is it?" he asked.

"It's a skateboarding video, sir. We're studying it in English."

"Skateboarding? In my day we studied my friend Shakespeare in English. Far more educational I would think."

"Can I, sir?"

"Can you what?"

"Use the AV room?"

"Okay, then."

Alex went inside and set up. He heard a tap on the window, quickly opened it and five Year 10's piled in. They had cans of coke and twisties, even though eating and drinking weren't allowed in the library. Kim threw Alex a Redskin.

Alex found it hard to fully enjoy the video as he was nervous that Mr Yates would walk in any second and go ballistic. Kim was right, though, it was sick. He couldn't believe it when a 17-year-old named Mark Appleyard pulled a nollie heelflip to boardslide down a long hand-rail. Alex was still learning how to do a normal boardslide, let alone attempting to nollie heelflip first.

The video showed the police hassling the skat-ers, and when a cop asked a boarder why he wasn't giving him any respect the boarder said, "You're talking to me like I'm an animal, not a human being."

"Amen," said Steve.

The bell rang and the Year 10s jumped out the window without being seen. Before she left, Alex noticed Kim drawing something on the wall with a red texta.

SWA

He got the hell out of there.

So this is the gang everyone is talking about. He wondered what it meant.

Outside he was relieved that they hadn't been busted. As he was walking back towards Block 2 John Carson-Zanger ran up to him. He was breathless. "I look for you everywhere," he said. "Jimmy and Billy big fight. Billy breaks Jimmy's nose."

Alex was shocked. "Where is he now?" he asked.

"Billy? In office."

"No, where's Jimmy?"

"In hospital."

Sarah Sceney was nearby getting books out of her bag. For a second her eyes met Alex's. She looked away.

CHAPTER 14
Jimmy Nose What He's Doing. Does Alex?

Jimmy was only at the Logan Hospital for a few hours. He had his nose packed to stop the bleeding and was examined by a doctor. "Plain as the nose in front of your face doesn't apply to you, does it, son?" the doctor said. "It should be 'plain as the nose sticking out the side of your face'." He laughed at his own joke.

Gently pushing and prodding, he waited until Jimmy started to relax then quickly snapped the nose back into place. Jimmy yelled. The doctor said it might remain slightly bent but not enough so that anyone would notice. Unless they looked real close, he said. He also said that Jimmy might feel woozy so it was best if he stayed home from school for a few days. Jimmy wasn't sure about no one noticing the bent nose but agreed on the importance of rest rather than school. He made a mental note to remember the doctor's name —

Chris Flicker. He might have to sue him in a few years.

Alex called Jimmy that night and asked what happened. Jimmy said he knew exactly what he was doing when he walked up to Billy and called him a low-life scumbag.

"How do you work that out?" asked Alex.

"I thought that getting flattened was the best way to find out how much Sarah cares."

"I can think of better ways. Like asking her."

"Yeah, well I s'pose I wasn't thinking straight. But I got my answer."

"She's visited you?"

"Nah. Not even a phone call. But at least I can stop worrying about her."

"Jimmy Homan — a single man again."

"Girls had better watch out."

"And they knowse it, too."

"Shut up, Jackson."

The next day Peter Callaghan was telling kids that Jimmy's face was so mangled he had to have plastic surgery, and that no one would recognise him when he returned to school. Adrian Dorry said Billy was let off with a warning, seeing as witnesses told the Year 9 coordinator that Jimmy had provoked him.

The Year 9 coordinator isn't as tough as Letch. Last year Alex and Billy were suspended for fighting by Mr Letcher — the Year 8 coordinator — no questions asked.

Without Jimmy at school, Alex started hanging out with the SWA gang. They sat at the same picnic table, shooting the breeze and passing Year 8s with pea-shooters. Alex told them what had happened to Jimmy, and Cookie, Nugget and Goof offered to beat Billy Johnstone up. Alex was tempted but said no. He thought things would settle down now that Billy and Jimmy had publicly aired their differences.

The group was certainly into their boarding. Kim had looked up some results on the Internet and saw that Casey came 10th in a vert competition in Switzerland. He won $1,000. They told Alex wicked stories about skateboarding on Friday nights down at Beeton. They had been chased by the police a few times, and last week a crazy shopowner got Steve in a headlock and sicked his dog onto him.

"We had to chuck rocks until he let Steve go," said Kim.

"At the dog?" asked Alex.

"Nah. The owner."

Alex wanted to check it out for himself. It sounded like there were great places to skate with lots of variety. Alex had boarded at the Beeton skatebowl so many times he could probably do it in his sleep. He actually did skate there in his sleep most nights, except when he dreamt about Becky. It would be good to try something new, even if it wasn't entirely legal.

He tried to think of ways he could convince his mum to let him go skateboarding with the group. He could think of only one: lie. Jimmy was back at school by the end of the week and agreed to help, though he thought Alex was crazy for wanting to skate downtown Beeton on a Friday night. "You want a nose like me?" he said.

The plan was that Alex would tell his mum he was staying with Jimmy, which was true. But he would skate until about 9 before going to his house. Alex's mum trusted him so there wasn't much chance she'd check the details with Mrs Homan. If she did he'd be dead meat.

"Don't forget that your oral presentations are due on Monday," said Mr Graham, "so now is a good time to do some last-minute preparations."

By period 6 on a Friday not many students are in the mood for last-minute preparations. "We'd better get this ready on Saturday," said Jimmy to Alex. "John, you have to talk for one minute about how the media portrays skateboarders in Romania."

"What's portrays?" he asked.

"You know … shows," said Jimmy.

"I don't know any skateboarders in Romania. Only gangsta rappers."

The bell rang and Alex told Jimmy he'd see him tonight.

"That's if you're not in hospital or jail," said Jimmy.

Alex felt nervous enough as it was. He didn't need his best mate making it worse.

CHAPTER 15
SWA

After school Alex rode to Kim's house and watched a skating video while the Year 10s shared a coke and a smoke. Kim's mum came in with a plate of lamingtons and the boys gobbled them up like poker machines. Alex found the way Kim and her mum talked to each other strange. It was like they were sisters, not mother and daughter.

"Did you buy some Bacardi today, Suz?" Kim asked.

"You're too young for alcohol."

"Yeah, and you're too old for that skirt. Did you?"

"Yeah."

"Cool. We'll have something to look forward to later."

They took off at about 5 and went down to the shops, starting on a five stair behind Red Rooster. It was a nice-sized ollie and there were soft bags of rubbish just past the landing zone. Kim needed them, crashing big-time when she tried to kickflip the steps. Steve nailed a sweet hardflip, and Alex landed sketchy on a backside 180.

They got chased away by an irate manager so they cruised to Bob Jane T-mart, where there was a one-metre gap between a thick wall and the carpark. It was about a two-metre drop, so it took guts to roll along the wall and ollie over the gap onto the carpark. Steve did it without even thinking, but the rest of the kids were happy to watch.

"You gonna do it, Jackson?" said Steve.

Alex was a little worried, but he popped it hard and made the distance. Just.

By this time everyone was hungry so they went down to Maccas, where Nugget's girlfriend, Jemma, worked. She snuck them free Fantas and fries and said she'd meet them at Kim's later for Bacardi. The group seemed to know heaps of people, including kids from Beeton High. Alex saw a kid he knew from primary school. The kid asked if Sarah Sceney still liked Alex.

"She hates my guts," Alex said.

"You must be stoked. That girl never left you alone. If I were you I would have used her then losed her. Hey, that's what you did, didn't ya?" the kid said, giving Alex a high five.

What's this kid on?

They cruised to the library. It looked different at night. A red light flickered eerily above the front door. Alex could see the computers inside, shut down.

There could be a message from Becky. It was strange how one piece of information could mean so much. A week ago Alex was feeling great about his relationship with Becky, and now he felt terrible. *One good message and it could all be okay.*

There was a large "NO SKATEBOARDING" sign above the front door. It didn't worry Kim, whose board smacked hard against the glass doors after she lost control of a frontside cess. Luckily, the glass didn't break. The library was closed but there were cleaners inside, and the loud noise made them look up and try and wave the kids away. Everyone ignored them except for Goof; he gave them the finger.

I'm glad Anne isn't inside.

There was a nice 3 flat 3 set of stairs and Steve ollied the whole six. He also pulled some nice 50–50s on the second marble stair. The marble was excellent for grinds, but grinds not so good for the marble. The entire edge of the bottom stair was chipped off. Maybe that's how the "NO SKATE-BOARDING" sign got there.

Alex did a 180 frontside flip down the first three stairs and then nollied the second three. He looked up but none of the guys saw it. Kim did, though, and she blew him a kiss.

Two of the boys found an old shopping trolley and with Nugget steering they attempted to jump it down 3 with Cookie inside. It landed on the front wheels and the trolley tipped forward, flipping Cookie onto the pavement. While everyone was laughing they heard an urgent call from Goof. "Cops!"

Everybody took off. Everybody except for Alex, who wasn't sure what to do. He froze like a kangaroo in front of a spotlight. A flashing blue spotlight. Two policemen ran towards him. "Stop!" they yelled.

"Go!" screamed Kim. Alex hesitated, then jumped on his board and bolted. He was about 10 metres behind the rest of the group and he could hear the policemen's footsteps as they ran up the marble steps. Alex followed the others as they skated past the library and then the courthouse. They were approaching a big set of stairs which led to the carpark. Past this were streets and alleys heading off in different directions.

The others had enough time to jump off their boards, run down the steps and jump back on in the carpark. Alex could still hear someone yelling behind him and he didn't want to slow down. He decided to ollie the set. He had plenty of speed so distance wasn't a problem, and luckily he landed it just right and skated off in a hurry.

Once they got beyond the carpark the police stopped chasing. Only when they rested behind the shops did Alex notice that his pulse was beating like an Uzi and his shirt was wet.

"Did you see that?" Kim said to the boys. "Alex popped it sweet down the courthouse steps!"

"How many are there again?" said Goof.

"Fifteen," said Kim. "And he did it easy. We should let him in, Steve."

"He was just skatin' scared," said Steve. "Next time we'll try it again, see if it was beginner's luck."

Alex wasn't sure he wanted there to be a next time.

"I say we let him in," said Kim.

"In what?" asked Alex.

"Our gang. SWA."

"What's it mean?"

"Kim!" warned Steve.

"He's all right, Steve." She looked at Alex. "Skateboarders With Attitude."

"No one gets in the first night," said Steve. "But you never know, the grommet might just have what it takes." He gave Alex a smile and Goof slapped him on the back.

"Good ollie, man."

Alex grinned. For one of the first times in his life he felt what it was like to belong to a group. Not like the reject soccer team he'd once played for or even the boys down the gym who he trained with in spurts. This was different. It meant something, though he wasn't sure why.

Kim smiled. "I'll tell you one thing, he won't forget tonight in a hurry."

CHAPTER 16
Bad Dreams

Alex passed on Bacardi at Kim's and went straight to Jimmy's. They pulled out the old mattress from under Jimmy's bed and Alex recounted the night's excitement. Jimmy couldn't believe that Alex had bolted from the police.

"You know there are video cameras all over Beeton. You'd better hope they don't go through the tapes," said Jimmy.

Alex started panicking at the thought of the police turning up at his house.

"Don't worry," said Jimmy. "Unless there's a camera at the library they can't prove it was you. Unless they took a hair or something and genetically matched it to yours."

"Can they do that?"

"Easy. But they'd only do it for something big. Like if you killed somebody."

Alex was exhausted, and he was almost asleep when Jimmy's voice floated quietly down.

"Why do you think she did it?"

"Who?"

"Sarah."

"Dunno. She's gone weird."

"It's like I'm not good enough for her anymore."

"You're too good for her."

There was another gap in the conversation, and Alex started drifting to another place. He was lost in those pretty brown eyes. He reached across and took her hand, and she leant in towards him, tipping her head so their noses wouldn't collide. Their lips met and she tasted different. More exciting, somehow. She felt different, too, and all of a sudden he knew why. It wasn't her. He sat up.

"You know, even though I hate his guts, I wouldn't mind being Billy Johnstone for a day," said Jimmy.

Alex must have been asleep for only a minute. "Why would you want to be that fool?"

"I don't know. Get any girl I want. Punch any boy I hate. It'd be fun I reckon."

"It's overrated."

"At least you know what it's like. I never will."

"You'll probably come up with a cure for cancer

one day. Or invent a really cool computer game," said Alex.

"Yeah, but I'll still be a red-headed geek."

"It could be worse," said Alex.

"How?"

"You could be John Carson-Zanger."

They laughed. "You know, he's a pretty good guy," said Jimmy. "Weird, but okay."

"Why do you think the kids give him so much crap?"

"Well, he's Harry High Pants. And his English isn't too flash. But I reckon calling him a poof makes 'em feel good about themselves. Like, if he's getting it then they're not."

"Strange, hey?"

"Very."

"Night, He-man."

"Night, Michael."

It took Alex a long time to fall asleep. He wanted to see Becky clearly in his mind but he couldn't. It was like his brain had changed frequencies.

CHAPTER 17
Bad News

By the next morning Alex's stomach was as hollow as a Crazy Clark's Easter egg. At 9 o'clock Jimmy was still dead to the world so Alex left, buying himself a packet of Twisties on the way to the library. Anne was at the front desk.

"Alex," she said, "the cleaners have been complaining about skateboarders coming here at night. You wouldn't happen to know who they are?"

He hesitated for a moment, then shook his head. "Probably Beeton High kids."

He checked his email and there were two new messages from Becky.

To: **alexjackson@skunkmail.com.au**
From: **beckyt13@hotmail.com**
Dearest Alex,
Hello! Thanks for writing back so soon. You're the best! But I probably

shouldn't tell you that. You might get cocky.

I can't believe Sarah cheated on Jimmy! She must have really changed. She used to be so nice. I'm going to email her and ask her what the hell is going on.

I'm not sure whether you should tell Jimmy. Sometimes I think it is better not to find out if something like this happens. It would hurt too much. Especially if the person is really sorry and won't do it again. Still, knowing Billy he'll tell everyone, so maybe you should tell him. I don't know. I'm sure you'll do what is right.

Guess what? My mum is going to take me to Trieste to watch Casey skate the weekend after next. (Trieste is a pretty Italian city on the border of Slovenia. It is on the Adriatic Sea, so it is a bit like the Gold Coast.) This weekend I am going skiing with my friend again, so I'm getting to travel heaps. Not much time for homework, but that's okay.

Sorry it sounded like I was down about us in my last email. I didn't mean to be. Of course I don't want us to break up. I just think we have to be realistic. There is a good chance that one or both of us will meet someone else. I know it is sad but it's the truth. I just hope we can stay really good friends if it does happen. If you wrote and said you had met someone else I would want to keep being your friend and still write to you. Do you feel the same way? I would be so sad if you said you never wanted to write or talk to me again if we broke up.

Well enough of this sad stuff. Let me know how everything went with Sarah and Jimmy. How's skateboarding? Remember not to get any scars. I want you to keep your good looks for the next time I see you.

Love,
Becky.
XXXX
PS. Say hi to Sam and Mandy for me. Tell them I haven't found any Italian boys for them yet, but I'll keep looking.

To: **alexjackson@skunkmail.com.au**
From: **beckyt13@hotmail.com**
Dear Alex,
I went to check my email today and you haven't written back. I think it is the first time ever! Are you just busy or is something wrong? I hope you're not mad at what I wrote about the possibility of us breaking up. Don't

be. You know I like you heaps and heaps. More than that.
 Hope to hear from you (very) soon.
Love always,
Becky.

Alex knew he had to reply. He sat at the computer for a long time, trying to figure out what to say. In the end he went for the direct approach.

To: **beckyt13@hotmail.com**
From: **alexjackson@skunkmail.com.au**
Dear Becky,
Are you cheating on me with a bloke called Roberto?
Alex
PS. Don't lie.

On his way out of the library Alex checked for video cameras. He couldn't see any. He also counted the courthouse steps. Kim was right, there were 15, and it was a humungous ollie. He wasn't sure he'd have the guts to try it without some help from the boys in blue. There was a nice-height handrail beside the steps as well, and Alex could see that it was all scratched. *Steve?*

He got home and Chief was on his way out to

the car with his boxing gear. There were gloves, tape and a first aid kit.

"Have a good night, champ?" Chief asked.

Alex's stomach tightened. "What?"

"At the Homan's place. Good night?"

"Oh yeah. Not bad. Ben fighting today?"

"Yep. He's taking on the Queensland Champion from the weight division up. Should be a good fight."

"Coach well, Chief."

"Always do."

Alex called out as Chief started up the old sigma.

"When do you leave for Russia?"

"Two weeks."

"You and Mum talking yet?"

He shook his head.

Inside Sam was dressed up in a red hipster skirt and crop top.

"Another party?" Alex asked.

"The Hyperdome," said Sam. "Seeing a movie."

"Can I come?"

"Don't be stupid. I'm meeting kids from school."

"Afraid I'll cramp your style? You got a boyfriend yet?"

"Have you met any Year 7 boys lately?" said Sam. "They are so immature."

"You want me to introduce you to some high school guys?"

"I wouldn't go out with Jimmy if you paid me," said Sam.

"Jimmy's all right. And he's not the only friend I've got."

Her expression softened. "Yeah, I heard something about you hanging out with some hotties at Maccas last night?"

"Who told you that?"

"I have my sources. So who are they?"

"Your sources are clueless. I was at Jimmy's last night."

"I can get Mum to check with Mrs Homan if you like?"

"Sam! Don't!"

"Then don't lie. And bring those guys around some time."

"They're not your type."

"How do you know my type?"

"They're in Year 10."

"I like mature guys."

Alex rolled his eyes and left. As he went into his room the photo on his desk caught his eye. He and

Becky looked so happy — she on his lap with her arm around his shoulders, his arm around her waist. It was only six weeks ago, and now they were on the rocks.

He thought about what she wrote. Would he still want to be friends with her if they broke up? If she told him she was going out with a fool called Roberto? If she was sneaking into his room during their skiing holidays, wrapping those long arms around him as their lips met …

He threw the photo into the bottom of his underwear drawer. *Not bloody likely.*

CHAPTER 18
The Nightmare Continues

On Monday Chief dropped Alex off at school, raving about Ben's fight. Ben knocked the guy out with a left hook "as good as any punch I've seen by an amateur", he said.

Chief was on his way into town to organise stuff for the trip. Alex could tell he was starting to get nervous. Chief had only been overseas once — on his honeymoon with Sharon to Vanuatu. The day they were meant to fly home he lost his passport, plane tickets and all their money.

"Ready for today, fellas?" asked Mr Graham as he walked past Alex and Jimmy before morning bell.

"You know us, sir. We're always ready," said Jimmy.

"Good to hear. You can go first then."

First for what?

Alex and Jimmy looked at each other. It was hard to tell which face turned white first.

"The presentation is today!" said Alex.

"Oh, shiiiivers," said Jimmy.

"Did you put it on PowerPoint?" asked Alex.

"Forgot. Did you bring the video?"

"It's at home."

"We're stuffed."

They quickly found John. At least he said he was prepared.

"You said talk one minute about Romania," said John.

"About skateboarding in Romania," said Jimmy.

"Of course."

"Will your bit be any good?" asked Jimmy.

"Not good. Great."

"Well, you're going first then."

Jimmy and Alex made a plan. Jimmy would write his part during double Tech studies in periods one and two. Alex would try and get hold of a skateboarding video. Hopefully, they could do enough to pass.

At recess Alex found Kim and luckily she had a video in her bag.

"It's a real good one, too," she said. "Make sure you watch the start."

As they walked into English, Alex prayed for a fire drill. A real fire, even.

"How's it going?" he asked Jimmy.

"Shocking," Jimmy said. "I'd written two pages when Mullet confiscated it. Wouldn't give it back to me after class, either."

Mullet was the nickname given to Mr Relf — the technology studies teacher — on account of a haircut he'd had last year. As soon as he found out about the nickname he'd changed his hairstyle — but the name had stuck.

Mr Graham lived up to his word and made Alex, Jimmy and John go first. As they stood up at the front Alex felt his insides churn like a milkshake. Ollieing down the courthouse steps was hard, but doing an English oral without preparation was near impossible. Before they started, Jimmy handed him a palm card.

"What's this for?" Alex asked.

"When you can't think of anything to say, look down," said Jimmy.

"But there's nothin' on it."

Jimmy shrugged.

Jimmy introduced the presentation. "Umm, to-day we are going to speak about the attitude of skateboarders. John will start by talking about how skateboarding is portrayed in Romania. I will tell you about a skateboarder I know. And Alex will analyse a skateboarding video for you. After this talk you should have a very good idea about skateboarders and how they are shown by the media and stuff."

John took a few confident steps forward. "Skateboarding in Romania is seen by media as popular not. Skateboarders usually get beaten up, so they don't have good attitude. Rapping is much better. Eminem, Tupac, Dr Dre, Snoop Doggy Dog — all famous in Romania. One day I want to be famous rapper. I rap like this:

> I take out my biscuit coz I'm prepared to risk it
> If I'm caught by the cops, my AK-47 will make 'em
> stop …

When John finished his rap he summarised his powerful argument. "So you see, skateboarders in Romania are shown as bad by media. Rappers are good. I'm finished now."

He stepped back to let Jimmy take over. He looked over at Alex. "How I do?" he whispered.

Jimmy looked down at his blank palm card. "Umm, I am going to tell you a story about a skateboarder I know. His name is Al … an. Once he was content with going to the skatepark and mastering lots of impressive tricks. He was awesome, probably the second best skater in the whole park. He did it because he loved skateboarding. Now he has joined a gang called SWA and they skate downtown Beeton on Friday nights. Last Friday he even got chased by the police. If my friend isn't careful, he could get into lots of trouble."

Jimmy looked at his palm card again.

"I think my friend should skate because he likes it. Not for the thrill of doing bad things."

He stepped back, and Alex gave him a dirty look. Jimmy shrugged. "I couldn't think of anything else to say," he said.

The video came on and Alex watched it closely. Like the rest of the class, this was the first time he had seen it.

It began with a boarder mooning a group of schoolgirls from the back of a tour minibus and went downhill from there. There were obscene gestures, obscene language, and obscene music. After a minute Mr Graham got up and pushed the eject button.

"I hope you have a very good reason for showing us this," he said.

Alex cleared his throat, looked down at his palm card, and cleared his throat again. "Skateboarding, umm, represents the youth of today. The youth of today are angry. Everybody always tells them what to do. When the guy mooned the girls …"

Some kids giggled.

"… he was doing something that wasn't, like, acceptable. He was doing something that might get him into trouble. Taking risks is what skateboarding is all about. So what the video is showing is how skateboarders really act … well, some of them."

Alex looked down at his palm card again, but he couldn't think of anything else to say.

"I'd like to see you boys after class," said Mr Graham. "And please show me all your notes and palmcards."

Teachers at St Joey's have different ways of getting students into trouble. Some yell, to make the student feel embarrassed. This feeling usually lasts only a few seconds, until the kid whispers something like "old fart" under his breath as the teacher walks away. Some teachers, though, take a different approach. If they do it right, they can make the student feel bad all day.

"I'm very, very disappointed in you boys. I expected much more, especially from you, Alex and Jimmy. What happened? Your ten-minute presentation went for three minutes, and it looked like you had no idea what you were doing."

100

Alex shrugged.

"I asked what happened?"

"Alex and I forgot about it, sir," said Jimmy.

"You had three weeks to prepare and you forgot about it?"

"Yes sir," Jimmy mumbled.

"Didn't you find this topic interesting, Alex?" Mr Graham asked.

"Yes sir."

"Then why didn't you make a better effort?"

"Umm, dunno. Busy, I s'pose."

"Busy getting yourself into trouble, according to what Jimmy said."

"I was talking about someone else," said Jimmy.

"Mmm, I see. Well I have no option other than to fail you."

"Fail?" said John. "My mum kill me."

"Can't you give us another chance, sir?" said Jimmy. "We promise we won't stuff up this time."

"I don't think so."

"C'mon sir, please?" Jimmy put on his best hangdog look, his top lip quivering slightly. He saved this look for special occasions. The last time Alex saw it was when Jimmy was practising casting his fishing-line in the backyard and accidentally hooked the neighbour's cat.

Mr Graham sighed. "I'll let you boys give the presentation again, next week. At the moment you've failed, but if you do an excellent job I might raise your grade to a C. Prove to me and yourselves that you are better than this."

"Thank you, sir."

"And no obscene video footage, okay?"

"Yes, sir."

"And John. No rapping."

Outside Peter Callaghan and Adrian Dorry were waiting for the inside scoop. "What did Graham say?" Peter asked.

"Said we failed," said Jimmy. "We gotta do it again next week. If we do good we can still pass."

"Don't worry," said Adrian. "The girls are doing a speech about the bloke who wrote *Romeo and Juliet*, and I heard that Sarah Sceney got a D+."

"That's impossible," said Jimmy.

"It's true. Emma Barney told me."

"I know that movie," said John. "Leonardo di Caprio and Claire Danes. They meet at fishtank. Who wrote it?"

"James Cameron," said Peter.

"Nah, it's an old guy," said Jimmy. "William Skatesbeard or something."

"Mr Yates is friends with him," said Alex. "He told me about him the other day."

"He must be old if he knows Yatesy," said Peter. "He's been librarian for, like, 50 years."

"Well, I hope we don't have to study him," said Adrian. "If Sarah failed it must be hard. She's a nerd."

"She was until she kissed Billy," said Peter. "He sucked her brains out through her tongue."

"Shut up, Callaghan," said Jimmy.

CHAPTER 19
Interrogated by Letch

The fog of secrecy that surrounded SWA was slowly being lifted, at least for Alex. Though not an official member he was now on the inside. "What my brother taught me," Steve said, "is that we can't trust anyone in authority. Teachers, cops, judges — they all exist to keep us in our place. To keep us down. We started SWA to stand up for ourselves."

"Why don't you just talk to them?" said Alex.

"Who?"

"The teachers and cops."

"They don't listen. But we're going to make 'em listen. And skateboarding is our microphone."

"Come along on Friday," Kim said. "We're gonna make you part of our gang."

"Yeah, we can use a grommet like you," said Steve. "People listen when you've got something they want. All of us skate hard. Every kid in the school wants to be like us."

"Soon, every kid in the school will know us," said Kim. "We're going to be famous."

"Infamous more like it," said Steve with a grin.

* * *

Each afternoon Alex stopped by the library, and each day he became more frustrated that Becky hadn't written back. *If nothing was going on, surely she would have denied it by now?*

At home Chief was almost ready for his big trip. He asked Alex to read him the travel list that Queensland Boxing had given him.

"Passport and plane tickets?" said Alex.

"Check," said Chief.

"Travellers cheques in US dollars?"

"Check."

"I said cheques."

"Very funny."

"Seven sets of training clothes, including socks, underwear and the team tracksuit?"

"Check."

"Boxing kit, including first aid stuff?"

"Check."

"A very warm jacket."

"Check. I've got my 80s leather jacket."

"A new brain so you won't forget everything?"

Alex had to skip away when Chief tried to punch him in the stomach.

* * *

Kim and Steve were right. At school on Friday everybody was talking about SWA. Their initials were sprayed across the Block 4 wall — in humungous writing. Not only that but they had left a message addressed to the school principal:

DEAR MR STAHL
IT'S OUR TIME NOW
SWA

The outside clock — donated by the police and proudly hung at the top of the Block 4 wall — was gone. It looked like someone had scaled 10 metres clinging to the outside drainpipe to get it down. A crazy thing to do unless your name was Spiderman. The school was taking the theft seriously — two police had arrived and were inspecting the scene. Alex thought he recognised one of them from Friday night. He slipped to the back of the crowd. Dozens of kids were milling around, talking about SWA.

"It stands for Satan Worshippers Association," said Peter Callaghan.

"No, it's Students who Want Acceptance," said a Year 11 girl. "The nerds are striking back."

A Year 10 boy spoke up. "It's Skateboarders With Attitude, you idiots. You know, Steve and the gang."

"Good on 'em," said another student.

"Yeah, sucked in, Mr Stahl," said someone else. "When does he ever listen to what we want?"

Later in Religion, while Alex was trying to figure out the difference between Paul and Saul, the classroom phone rang.

"Alex, you are wanted in the office," said Mr Bath. "Go forth young man and speak the truth."

The truth was what worried him.

He walked into the office expecting to see Mr Dowden, but instead was face to face with Letch.

"ALEX, DO YOU KNOW WHY YOU ARE HERE?"

Letch had two volumes. Loud and louder.

"No sir."

"HAVE YOU SEEN THE DISGRACEFUL ACT OF THEFT AND VANDALISM IN OUR SCHOOL?"

"You mean the clock?"

"AND THE GRAFFITI."

"Yes sir."

"MR DOWDEN IS AWAY FOR A FEW DAYS SO I WILL BE GETTING TO THE BOTTOM OF IT. I'LL ASK YOU AGAIN, WHY ARE YOU HERE?"

"Because you rang me up in religion, sir."

Letch's voice went up a few decibels.

"ARE YOU PLAYING GAMES WITH ME, SON?"

"No sir."

"DID YOU HAVE ANYTHING TO DO WITH WHAT HAPPENED?"

"No sir."

"DO YOU KNOW ANYTHING ABOUT THIS SWA GANG?"

Alex hesitated for a second.

"No sir."

"DO YOU KNOW WHAT SWA MEANS, ALEX?"

"I'm not sure, sir. I've heard some kids say it means Satan Worshippers Association."

"WELL, I'VE HEARD IT MEANS SKATE-BOARDERS WANTING ATTITUDE. I'VE ALSO HEARD THAT YOU MIGHT HAVE SOME SORT OF LINK WITH THIS GROUP. IS THAT TRUE, ALEX?"

Alex looked down.

"IS IT TRUE?"

He looked straight at Letch. "I don't know anything about it."

Letch stared at him. Alex felt like there was a flashing sign across his forehead that said "LIAR".

"I have always found you to be truthful, Alex," he said, more quietly. "I hope there is no reason for me to change my opinion of you."

"Yes sir."

"Yes, there is a reason?"

"I mean, no sir."

Steve was sitting on the chair outside and he winked as Alex walked past. Alex couldn't believe it. He looked as cool as a Kelvinator.

"Alex," Letch called out.

"Sir?"

"How's Becky doing in Italy?"

"Umm, I'm really not sure, sir."

"I'm sorry to hear that."

As Alex walked back to class he could hear Letch interrogating Steve. Probably the whole school could. "HOW DARE YOU SMIRK AT ME LIKE THAT, BOY!"

After school the gang went straight to Kim's place. Alex had told his mum the same story about staying at Jimmy's house, and although she wasn't keen, she eventually agreed. Jimmy also wasn't keen.

"If you keep playing with fire, mate, you're gonna get burned," he said.

"Yeah, especially when someone's mate lights the match."

"I told you, I couldn't think of anything else to say."

"Well, you could have changed the initials at least. Why did you have to use SWA?"

"How was I supposed to know they were going to flog the school's clock? I can't believe you want to be a skateboarder with attitude, anyway. It's such a stupid name."

"Shut up, bent nose."

At Kim's they cross-checked the day's events. Everyone except Goof had been called up to the office and questioned about the incident. They all had denied it, of course. Goof felt left out.

"When did you steal the clock?" Alex asked.

"The less you know, the better," said Steve. "We'll all be questioned again, I reckon, when Dowden gets back."

"You did well, Alex," said Kim, blowing out a steady stream of smoke. "I bet that's the first time you've ever been in trouble."

"No, it's not."

"First time you've ever had to lie, then."

He paused. "Are we going skating or what?"

CHAPTER 20
Initiation

The skateboarders with attitude were on a high as they cruised around Beeton that night. They all ollied the gap at Bob Jane T-Mart and Alex kick-flipped over a garden wall from the top of a five-stair.

At McDonald's kids from St Joey's asked them about the missing clock. "How'd you climb up so high?" a girl said. "I think what you did is cool," said a Year 12 boy. "Stuff the school and stuff the police."

No one in the group admitted to stealing anything. But it didn't stop them basking in the glory.

"If the school stopped fearing us and listened to our needs then this wouldn't happen," said a pumped-up Goof.

"What do you want the school to do?" asked the girl.

He thought for a few seconds. "Umm, they

could, like, play headbangin' music at lunchtime. And build a half-pipe at the school. That'd kick!"

Kim took over. "They should treat us like human beings. All the teachers ever say to me is 'pull your socks up', 'take your earrings out'. They should stop treating us like we're little kids and give us the freedom to be individuals."

"Go girl!" said Goof.

Over free fries, courtesy of Jemma, Steve told Alex what it meant to be a member of SWA. "We all look out for each other. I would spill blood for anyone in the gang, and they would do the same for me. You are either in or out — no in-between."

This was sounding heavy. "And if you're in SWA you have to skate your arse off," Steve said, grinning. Alex knew he could do that.

They cruised down to Beeton State School — Alex's old primary school. It brought back memories. He could see the window he once broke with a mis-timed kick of the soccer ball. There was the brick wall that he and Jimmy had waged legendary bashball battles on. They skated in the undercover area where Sarah Sceney once told the whole school assembly that she loved him.

Kim was having fun trying pop shove-its down a three-stair and Steve was grinding and sliding everything in sight. Goof, Nugget and Cookie were finishing off their burgers, and afterwards tossed the wrappers onto the ground. Alex remembered how his group of Year 7s would tell off the younger kids when they did this. Even though Beeton was a poor school, they were proud of it.

After an hour Steve suggested they head to the courthouse.

"Isn't that risky?" Alex said.

Even Kim looked doubtful. "I don't have much money, Steve. I can't afford another 80 buck fine."

"Then don't get caught," Steve said. "The courthouse is where Alex is having his initiation."

Initiation?

Once they arrived Steve told Goof to keep a look-out for the police. His voice was soft and serious as he spoke to Alex.

"Whenever a new member is initiated into SWA, they have to face fear and kick it in the guts. Fear is what keeps you down. I've seen my brother do incredible things on a skateboard because he had no fear. I've climbed up walls, boardslided down rails because I don't give a stuff. I want you to feel the same way. Ollie down the 15. Show us that last week wasn't a fluke."

"You can do it, Alex," said Kim.

"Come on, grommet," said Cookie, "show us what you're made of."

Alex took a look down the steps and felt his stomach tighten. It was a long way down. If he landed wrong he could snap an ankle. If he had to bail, it could be worse.

Don't think.

He skated back to position. He wondered what Casey would say if he was here. *If Casey was here would I be doing this?*

Alex thought about whether he really wanted to join SWA. He still didn't know what to make of Steve, though he had to admit Steve was a great boarder. The other guys were okay, though different from his usual friends. This gang stuff wasn't like him, but for some reason he wanted to be here. He felt accepted, part of something. And there was something else, something he didn't like to admit.

Don't think.

He pushed off hard. He needed speed to clear the 15 and the last thing he wanted was to land on the stairs. The skateboard was loud against the slate tiles, but as he bent down to ollie he heard Kim's voice. "You can do it!"

No I can't. He did a backside cess at the last

instant, skidding to a halt a centimetre from the top step.

"Just measuring my take-off," he said to the others.

Kim came up to him. She put her hands on his shoulders. "You're an awesome skater, Alex, maybe even better than Steve. I know you can make it."

She ran down the steps and when she got to the bottom she stopped. She turned and gave Alex a smile, then lay down on the bottom step.

"Kim, you don't have to do that," Steve said.

She didn't answer.

"Kim, move!"

She didn't.

Alex was ready again and this time there was no chickening out. He made sure he got plenty of speed so he wouldn't give Kim a facial on the way down. He popped the ollie hard, and grabbed the board with his right hand to keep it steady. Flying down those 15 steps seemed to take forever, yet in another way it was over before he knew it.

He caught just a glimpse, but even later he could see her clearly. Her eyes were closed but her face soft and peaceful. She looked like a child sleeping in the back of a car on a stormy night. Would Becky have had as much faith in him? Missing

Kim's nose by about 10 centimetres, he landed perfectly on the bitumen.

He heard Cookie scream "You the man!" and Kim draped her arms around him and squeezed.

"You did it!" she said.

"You said I would."

"How do you feel?"

"Relieved. I thought I was going to land on your face."

"Well you didn't. Lucky for you I'm still beautiful." She laughed and kissed his cheek.

Steve said he was going to ollie the 15 and he asked Kim to lie on the bottom step for him as well. She said she'd had enough excitement for one night.

"Don't you trust me?" he said.

"I'll do it," said Nugget. "I trust you."

Steve missed Nugget's gut by a good 30 centimetres and landed nice. Alex couldn't believe how relaxed Steve looked on the way down, like he was in total control.

"Let's celebrate Alex joining SWA," said Kim. "Suz bought some rum."

"Soon," said Steve. "Alex has to do one more thing. We knew he would clear the stairs. We saw him do it last week. To be initiated into SWA you have to do something that you're really scared of."

"Yeah, I had to let the air out of a cop car's tyres," said Goof. "I nearly crapped myself."

"What else can I do?" asked Alex. "Run with the bulls?"

"Boardslide it," he said, gesturing towards the rail that ran down the stairs.

"You're crazy," said Alex.

"Listen." His voice became serious. "You're a top skater. Nearly as good as me. I wouldn't ask you to do it if I didn't think you could. My brother did it when he was in Year 9. So did I. You can do it too. You just have to not be scared."

"Have you really done it?" asked Alex. Board-sliding down 15 stairs was enough to get you a start on a skateboarding video, and even the pros some-times slammed trying it.

"I'll prove it," he said.

"Steve, let's go home," said Kim. "We don't need this tonight."

"Kimmy, don't be such a girl."

Steve ran up the steps and flicked his baggy shirt up by the shoulders. His sagging pants were half-way down his bum, showing off his red boxers. And then he pushed off, before any of them had time to think about what a crazy thing he was doing. He didn't even look worried, like he was having a relaxing Sunday skate.

Is this bloke scared of anything?

Steve ollied up onto the rail and turned his hips 90 degrees backside, landing on the middle of his Hardcore deck. He was sliding down the rail fast but smooth when Alex noticed everything was flashing bright blue.

As Steve flew off he twisted his hips to straighten the board, but something stuffed up. Perhaps he twisted a fraction early, or maybe there was a bump in the rail, but the back wheel got caught. Steve flew at the bitumen without a board to land on and he bounced, rolled, and bounced again. Blood started streaming from about four parts of his body, but he got straight up and ran over to his board. He picked it up and chucked it as hard as he could. It landed smack on the bonnet of a cop car.

CHAPTER 21
Busted

By the time Alex arrived at her place, Kim was the only one of the gang still there. Goof felt bad about not noticing the police car and took off. Cookie went looking for him, and Nugget went to see Jemma. Steve, well, he hadn't shown up. Probably still at the station.

"What happened?" Kim asked Alex.

"They arrested Steve. Put him in the back of the cop car and drove off."

"Did he go sick?"

"Not at first. The policewoman asked him his name and he said, 'Tony Hawk', but the policeman knew who Steve was. Then he started saying all this stuff and Steve totally lost it."

"Did the pig yell at him?"

"Nah, it was weird. He was acting real nice. He said he went to school with Steve's brother, Ryan, and that he was a good bloke. He said he didn't want the same thing to happen to Steve that happened to his brother. Then Steve started yelling at the cop, telling him to shut up. And then he started bawling. That's when they drove Steve away."

"Steve cried?"

"Yep."

"I need a drink," she said.

Alex followed Kim to her bedroom. The walls were packed with dark sketches and paintings. Becky was a talented artist, but comparing this art with Becky's was like comparing KOЯN to Matchbox 20. Becky drew beautiful landscapes, Kim drew … weird stuff. And lots of it.

One painting stood out. On one half everything was as you'd expect — a family portrait in the front yard. There were big smiles, a beautiful house and a friendly dog. The other half was a mirror image, except the mirror was demented. The windows were broken and the front door had an axe through it; the father had the face of a monster and the rest of the family looked terrified. And the dog was dead.

"That's what won me the art competition," she said. "It's called 'Illusion of the Family'."

Alex took a closer look. It was beautiful and

scary at the same time. "Has anyone ever told you you've got issues?"

She handed him a drink.

He shook his head. "I'm not 18."

"Neither am I. It'll calm you down."

The rum was bitter in his mouth. It tasted bloody awful, actually, but after a few gulps his head relaxed and his throat felt hot.

"What'd the cops do to you?" she asked.

"They gave me this." He held up a ticket for $80.

"Did you give 'em a fake name and address?"

"Yeah. I can't believe I did it. I told 'em I was Billy Johnstone."

"Good one."

He looked at her. "Hey Kim, what did the policeman mean about Steve ending up like his brother?"

She looked down at her drink. "Why'd you stay with Steve, anyway?"

"I thought we'd all stay," Alex said. "Steve said you'd spill blood for him."

"Steve spilt enough blood for one night. There was nothing we could do."

"I just thought someone should stay," he mumbled.

She looked at him. "Tell me something. Would you have done it?"

"Done what?"

"Boardslided the 15."

He shook his head. "Doubt it."

She moved closer, pouring more rum into his glass. Their legs were touching. "I bet you would have, hey?"

"Dunno."

"You would have. You'd have done it for me."

It was different from his times with Becky. He was more relaxed, confident even, and he eased Kim back onto the bed as their lips met. At first the rhythm was slow but it became faster, more urgent. Alex's head was swimming from the alcohol, or maybe it was something else. Kim slipped her hand underneath his shirt and rubbed his chest with her fingertips. He knew he was out of his depth but he didn't want to stop. Her hand went down to his stomach, and in a rush he felt his desire slip away.

She smiled. "You're not very experienced, are you?"

"At skateboarding, yes. Girls, no."

He went to the bathroom and when he came back Kim had her arms around another boy. It was Steve. He pulled away when he saw Alex.

"Hey grommet," he said. "I didn't know you were …"

"Alex came to tell me what happened," Kim said.

Steve looked tired and pale, his skin raw on his knees, elbow and the side of his face. "Thanks for hanging around," he said to Alex. "More than I can say about some people."

Kim looked away.

"They let you go?" said Alex.

"Mum came and got me. I'm charged with wilful damage of a police car. I didn't even see the bloody thing."

"What's going to happen?"

"Nothin' much. Go to court next month. I'm still 15, thank Christ."

Alex looked down at his watch and saw that it was almost midnight. "I've gotta go," he said.

He waited for Kim to give some sort of cue, but none came. "See ya, then."

"Hey grommet," said Steve, coming up to him. "You're in."

"In what?"

"SWA."

He slapped Alex's hand and looked him in the eye. "You did good tonight. Next week we'll go back to the courthouse and boardslide the mother."

Alex shook his head. "You are crazy."

Kim squeezed in between them and put an arm around each of their shoulders. "I think you both are."

This was the signal Alex was waiting for. He leant in and gave Kim a kiss goodnight. It was only after he did it that he realised she didn't reciprocate. In fact, she had tried to pull away.

"Hey, you two haven't …?" Steve raised his eyebrows. "You have, haven't you? Well, you really are a member of the gang now, grommet."

"Shut up, Steve," said Kim.

* * *

Alex was still trying to figure out what Steve meant as he turned into Jimmy's street. He stopped worrying, not because it no longer bothered him but because he suddenly had more important things on his mind. The red Sigma was parked in the Homan's driveway and leaning against the boot was Chief.

Busted.

CHAPTER 22
Fighting Chief

"Out," said Alex when Chief asked him where he'd been.

"Doing what?"

"Skateboarding."

Chief looked at his watch. "Skateboarding at midnight?"

Alex shrugged.

"Who with?" said Chief.

"Kids from school."

Chief stopped leaning on the car and stood up stiffly. "What else you been doing?"

"Nothin'."

"You been drinking?"

"No."

"Come here," he said.

"What?"

Chief moved forward and grabbed him by the

shoulders. He pulled him close. "I can smell it," he said. "You taking drugs?"

"No!"

Grabbing him around the cheeks Chief looked into his eyes. Alex fought to get away but Chief's strong arms had him pinned. Alex lashed out, kicking him on the shin.

Chief pushed him away. His voice changed to the one he used at the gym when he had to keep the tough kids in line. "You wanna fight your dad now, champ? Well, come on. You're old enough to drink, stay out late. Let's see if you can whip your old man."

Alex was opening the car door when Chief stung him with a jab to the shoulder.

"You can lie to your mother, can't you champ? You think you're a man now? Well, prove it."

Alex threw a straight right at Chief's face. Chief instinctively leant back and the blow grazed past his nose. Alex started flailing punches at the body. Chief covered himself up with his elbows, but he didn't fight back. Alex kept punching, some of the shots getting through, but still Chief didn't retaliate. Alex's arms became heavier and heavier — the punches turning into slow motion — and then they gave out, hanging loosely by his sides. Instead of giving him a beating, Chief put his big arms around Alex and held him close.

"Talk to me, son."

"What do you care? You spend more time with Ben than you do with me," Alex said, the tears stinging his eyes. "I hope you stay in Russia forever."

CHAPTER 23
Slammed

That night Sharon let him off the hook but made her intentions clear. "In the morning we talk. And I expect the truth."

He nodded.

"Say it."

"We'll talk."

"And?"

He sighed. "I'll tell the truth."

On his way to bed Alex couldn't help but have a dig at Sam. "Thanks for spilling your guts."

"You're so stupid sometimes."

She said it without the usual fire in her voice. Alex looked closer. Her shoulders were hunched and her chin sagged.

"What's wrong?"

"It's been bad. Mum and Dad were yelling at each other."

"What'd they say?"

"Mum was blaming Beeton, and Dad said it didn't have anything to do with it. He said that you're learning how to become a man or something. Then Mum said that you'd learn more if you had a better role model. After that Dad drove off."

"At least they were talking."

She looked at him. "What's happened to you?" Alex could see the lines on her face from where she had been crying. "Are you going through puberty or something?"

Alex looked down. Without even trying he was hurting his friends, his family. He wanted things to be right. At least with someone. He made his voice start low and then crack at the end of the sentence. "No I'm noooot."

Sam tried to stay mad but she couldn't. They laughed and laughed until tears were running down their faces and their mum yelled at them to go to sleep.

"You might as well tell me what happened," said Sam, "coz you know I'll find out."

"Then it'd be no fun," he said. "How did Mum and Dad know I wasn't at Jimmy's?"

"Casey called from overseas. Mum gave him Jimmy's number, but when you weren't there Mrs

Homan called Mum back, all worried. You were caught out like a slimy toad."

"Did Casey say anything?"

"Dunno."

The next morning Alex slipped out early while everyone was still asleep. He knew it was risky but he had to see Kim. Thirty minutes later he stood outside her bedroom window and tapped on the glass.

The curtains finally opened and Kim's scrunched-up face appeared. She pointed to the back door. "What are you doing here?" she asked.

It was a good question. "I got busted by my parents," he said.

She shrugged.

"I'll probably get grounded till I'm 30. I wish they were cool like your mum," said Alex

"Suz is okay. She doesn't like me drinking and smoking and stuff, but she knows I'll do it anyway so she lets me. It was better when Dad was around. At least they could control me."

"You want to be told what to do?"

"No. Sometimes. I don't know. What are you doing here? Running away?"

"Nah. I just wanted to see you."

He reached for her hand but she took it away. "What's wrong?" Alex asked.

"Nothing. I just think you've got the wrong idea."

"About what?"

"About us."

He tried to think but his brain was fuzzy. If he said the right words, everything would be fine. He knew she liked him. "What about last night?"

"What about it?"

The way she said it was like a blow to the guts.

"Are you going out with Steve?" he said.

"I'm not going out with anybody."

"Do you sleep with him? Like last night after I left?"

"I don't have to listen to this crap. You can leave now."

He stepped out the door then turned. "I'm sorry, Kim. I didn't mean that. I just …"

He reached out again, but she shut the door.

* * *

He went to the skatepark. It was still early, so except for a little kid he was on his own. He dropped in from the vert a few times and thought of Casey. Alex missed him, especially his advice.

"Commitment is the key." Alex could see the railing tempting him, shining silver in the morning sun. It was time to face his fear and there didn't seem much to lose.

He ollied onto the rail easily, but something felt strange on the way down. Later he realised his back trucks were hooked in, so he was actually feeble grinding rather than sliding. Everything felt okay, however, until he went to pop off — when his back wheel got stuck. He flew forward and took the fall on his chest, his head raised and his arms out-stretched — like Superman. Also, like Superman, when he lifted up his shirt later that night, the rash made a letter across his chest. It wasn't an S, though. It looked a lot like an L.

When he hobbled back to his board the first thing he did was chuck it across the skatepark. Only when he looked up did he see that someone was sitting on one of the benches above the park watching him. It was his mum.

Also watching Alex was the little kid. He tried what was probably his first ever ollie, missed it, then chucked his board away in disgust.

"What are you doing here?" Alex said to his mother.

"What are you doing here, more like it? You know not to go out without our permission, especially after last night."

"So I'm a prisoner now?"

"No. But while you're living at our house you'll respect the rules. While I can't trust you you're not going out unsupervised."

"Chief never had rules when he was a kid and he turned out all right."

"He was lucky. Lots of his mates are either dead or in jail. I'm not going to have the same happen to you."

"I didn't even do anything that bad. I just skate-boarded with my friends."

"Maybe, maybe not. But you lied to me."

"If I'd told you the truth you wouldn't have let me go. I didn't want you to worry, that's all."

"So you were thinking of me?"

"Yes."

"Do you really believe that?"

"Yes."

"You *are* going through puberty."

They sat there for a minute, quiet. The little kid kept trying to ollie but he couldn't do it.

"I used to bring you down here, remember?" said Sharon. "You'd skate for ages, then come and sit next to me and we'd watch Casey. Remember what you'd say?"

"I'm gonna be as good as him one day."

"You were like that little kid. You'd keep trying a new trick until you could do it. I used to love watching you. And then when you'd finally do it you'd get mad if I didn't see."

He smiled. "I always did my best skateboarding when you had your head in a book."

"Sometimes I'd pretend I saw you, even when I didn't, just to see you smile. You were such a good boy," she said.

The kid was getting the hang of banging the tail on the ground but he was too slow sliding his front foot forward to get any air. His back wheels looked like they were glued to the concrete.

"I'm not now, am I?"

"No, you're not." She put her hand round his neck. "You're a fine young man. I know you'll find the right way, you always do. But your dad and I, we want to help you. We might not have been the greatest parents lately. You're turning into a man so fast."

Alex bit his lip. He was in danger of crying twice in two days. "It's not your fault I'm stuffing up," he said, "or Chief's. It's not Beeton's either."

"Whose is it?"

He couldn't answer. *Crybaby.*

The kid nailed one. He jumped as high as his

little legs would go, and his front foot caught the nose just in time to straighten it out and lift the back wheels off the ground. They only went up a centimetre or two, but to the kid it probably felt like he'd made it to the sky. He looked around to see if anyone had seen it, and Alex and Sharon gave him the thumbs-up. It was a new beginning.

CHAPTER 24
Moving to the Beach?

When they got home Chief wasn't there. "Why would he go out now?" said Sharon. "He'd better not be at another boxing tournament."

A few minutes later he rushed in. "So you finally found him?" Chief said. "Where was he, in the watchhouse again?"

"Please take this seriously, Jeff," said Sharon. "Where've you been?"

"I'll tell you later."

They sat around eating breakfast while Alex spilled his guts. Sharon asked most of the questions and Chief listened closely.

"So you've joined a gang?" said Sharon when Alex told them about SWA.

"Well … sort of. But it's not like we go around killing people."

"You just deface public property?"

"What's deface?"

"Wreck."

"Well, sort of."

Alex lived up to his promise and told the truth. He told them how he'd lied to Letch and the police. He told them about his problems with Becky, and even about Kim (though he left out a few details). Afterwards he felt surprisingly good. Like he'd taken a shower on the inside.

Chief said he had something to say to all of them. He yelled out to Sam, who popped up from behind the couch. "Just looking for something," she mumbled.

Chief cleared his throat. "Last night when Alex went walkabout, it hit me that I haven't been the best father or husband lately. You all know I love my job. Without boxing, and your mum here, of course, I would have turned out to be a bad apple, nothing surer. Training the boys is like helping kids who were just like me. I feel like they need me. But I love my family. And you need me, too. If you all think that living somewhere else will make us happier, then I've decided it's okay with me."

There was silence for a few moments. "Can we move to the beach?" said Sam.

"If that's what we all agree," said Chief.

"When would we go?" said Sam.

"Probably at the end of the year. That'd give us time to sell the house and for me to find a new job."

"What would you do?" asked Alex.

"I've been thinking I could work in a gym, run one of those boxercise programs."

"You mean a rich gym, not a boxing gym?"

Chief shrugged. "Well, what do you reckon about moving?"

Sam spoke up. "I think it'd be cool. As long as I could finish Year 7 at Beeton. I vote we go to the Gold Coast."

"Alex?" asked Chief.

He tried to weigh it up. St Joey's was okay, though his only real friend was Jimmy. And Casey wouldn't be hanging around Beeton much now that he had turned pro.

"I don't think you should change jobs," Alex said to Chief.

"Don't worry about me. What do you want to do?"

"I don't care," he said, finally. "I like it here but the coast would be okay, too, I s'pose. I could become a pro surfer."

"Well, we all know your mum has been saving money for us to move, so it looks like it's settled. I'll have to let them know down at the …"

"Wait," Sharon cut in. "I want to have my say. I think Alex is right."

I am?

"Jeff, you said that you've been selfish but so have I. I got all high and mighty just because I lost some jewellery. I expected you to give up your job, leave the place you grew up in, just so we could live in a nicer street, maybe buy a better car."

"One that didn't look so pov?" asked Sam hopefully.

"But Alex said that you should keep your job at the Boxing Club and he's right. You do great things for those boys. You give them a chance at a better life. And never once have you not been there for me or for the kids when we needed you. I would rather live with a happy husband in this place than with a miserable one in a mansion. There are more important things in life than money."

Chief reached into his pocket and pulled out a small case. He gave it to Sharon and she opened it. A tear ran down the edge of her cheek.

She slipped on the white diamond bracelet. "How …?"

"My boys went to every pawn shop in Logan City," said Chief. "Ben found it in Kingston. I went there this morning and bought it for you."

"You bought it? But it's mine!"

"I needed it straightaway," said Chief. "Plus, the guy gave me a pretty big discount."

For the first time in months Sharon took Chief's hand. He drew her to him and they kissed.

"Gross!" said Sam.

CHAPTER 25
Skateboarding Presentation: the Sequel

This time they were ready. They met on Sunday at Jimmy's place, brainstormed ideas and put the key phrases onto PowerPoint. After practising in front of the mirror they called it quits and introduced John to backyard cricket. He showed potential as a bowler and even got Alex out when a snick behind hit the back fence on the full. House rules.

Jimmy clean-bowled John off a ball which seamed viciously off a tuft of grass. "Howzaaaatttttt!!!!" he yelled.

"How is what?" said John.

The big day came and John got the presentation off to a more promising start than last time. He'd done his research and talked (rather than rapped) about how skateboarding was portrayed in Romania, and even had an article that (unfairly according to Alex and Jimmy) linked skateboarders to increased violence in Bucharest.

Jimmy put on his usual polished performance, explaining how the mainstream media made unfair generalisations about skateboarders, often using words like "gang" and "drug problem" when writing about their lifestyle. He then played Casey's video to show how skateboarders can be portrayed in a positive light. The class loved it, laughing at the part when Alex slammed, and cheering when Becky appeared.

Alex took a deep breath and stepped up to say his piece. "I can't tell you what skateboarding means to other people, but I can say what it means to me."

On the screen above him the word FREEDOM flew out.

"On a skateboard I am free. I can visit a mate, fly down a hill, or drop in from the vert. If I want to relax I can ride my board to the park and chill. If I want excitement I can ollie down a big set of stairs, though it's good to do this when the police aren't chasing you. To me freedom isn't about always doing what you want, it's …"

He paused as Jimmy pushed a button and the words flashed up on the screen, one by one:

LETTING GO OF FEAR

"Someone I know said that skateboarding is

about kicking fear in the guts. I reckon fear is the worst. When I'm skating well I feel like I can fly and I'm not scared of falling off. A lot of adults hate skateboarders because they are scared of them defacing public property. Some skateboarders hate the police because they are scared they'll bust them. I reckon that if everyone stopped being scared and tried to understand each other we'd all get along better. Without fear we'd be free."

The third and final point flew out letter by letter, as if shot by a gun:

LEARNING FROM YOUR MISTAKES.

"You all saw me fall off my board on the video. My friend Casey says that when you stack it you can either throw your board away or get back on and try again. I've done some pretty dumb things in my life, especially this year. Skateboarding teaches me that I should learn from my mistakes and get straight back on the board after a fall.

"So you see, skateboarding means a lot to me. It's not about being cool or disrespecting authority, it's about freedom, letting go of fear and learning from your mistakes."

The class gave a loud clap, then Mr Graham spoke. "Well, it looks like you listened to your own advice and learnt from your mistakes, boys, because that was a much better presentation. Well done."

* * *

At lunch Alex went to see SWA. They compared stories and Kim told the others how this Friday night Steve and Alex were going back to boardslide the courthouse stairs.

"That's fine by me," said Steve, "as long as Goof isn't the lookout."

The spray-painted message on the Block 4 wall had been scrubbed but was still visible, and a boy walking past gave SWA a clenched-fist salute.

"I can't go," said Alex. "I'm gonna stick to the skatepark for a while."

He knew it would come from one of them, most likely Steve, but he didn't expect it to be her. "Come on, grommet," Kim said. "Stop worrying about Mummy and Daddy and skate with us."

He shook his head.

"If you don't, you can't be in our gang."

Alex didn't answer.

The knife was in and she started to twist it. "You're scared of the rail, aren't you, grommet? Steve'll do it but you won't even try. You think you're a great skateboarder but you're not. You're a wuss."

Why are you doing this? First she pushed him away just as they were getting close, and now she was trying to hurt him as well. "We're all scared of something," he said. "It's just that some of us are too scared to admit it."

* * *

During lunch on Friday, Billy and Zane entertained the Year 9s. They pulled their pants up so high they gave themselves wedgies, and they began mimicking John — turning when he turned, scratching when he scratched. John pushed Zane to make him stop and he got pushed back twice as hard. Jimmy stepped in to support his mate.

"Give it a rest, losers," he said.

"John's bumchum is getting jealous," Billy said loudly.

A few kids giggled.

Jimmy didn't back down. "At least my bum doesn't have a giant A-hole sitting on top of it."

Kids laughed and then became quiet, anticipating some action.

Billy stepped towards Jimmy but someone stood in front of him. "Why don't you pick on something your own intelligence?" said Sarah Sceney. "Like an ant."

Billy went to grab her but stopped. It wouldn't do his reputation much good if he beat up a girl. "You weren't worried about my brain at Emma Barney's party," he said. "You had bigger things on your mind."

"Ooohhhh!" went a few boys.

"The only big thing you own is your ego," said Sarah. "At least Jimmy can kiss properly. You slobber like a dog."

"Oooohhh!" went the girls.

Both the boys and the girls then let out a loud cheer. Billy was dacked from behind by Claire Carney.

Jimmy gave Sarah a smile. There was something different but familiar about the way she looked.

Only later he realised she was wearing her glasses.

CHAPTER 26
Phone Call

Alex spent Friday night at home. Which was just as well or he would have missed Sam bringing her first-ever boy home for afternoon tea. For once Alex had the chance to embarrass her rather than the other way around.

"I heard you're a sick skateboarder," said Zac when Sam introduced them.

Maybe I'll go easy.

"Zac skateboards, too," said Sam. "He's real good."

"Not as good as Alex," said Zac, turning slightly red. "I heard you boardslided the courthouse stairs."

"Yeah, well don't believe everything you hear," said Alex, grinning.

Later that night Alex asked Sam if Zac was her boyfriend.

She smiled. "He's just a friend."

"He's a boy, isn't he?"

"Yes."

"And he's your friend?"

"Yeah."

"Well then he's your boy friend."

"Shut up."

The other thing Alex would have missed if he hadn't been home that night was a phone call from the other side of the world.

"G'day mate!" Casey said in a falsetto voice.

"Casey!" said Alex. "How's it going?"

"Really good," he said.

"How's the competition over there?"

"Hard. In the first few I kept getting disqualified for slamming, but I came 10th in Switzerland …"

"I heard."

"And I just won my first one last weekend in Trieste."

"That's awesome! How much did you get?"

"It was only small but I got two grand after tax. Better than nothing."

"Cool. Have you seen many good boarders?"

"I reckon," he said. "I met the flying monkey, Bob Burnquist, and you should see Rick McCrank on the street courses. He crushes them."

"Sick! When are you coming home?"

"Probably a month or so. I've snapped three decks since I've been here so I'm short of gear. A couple of teams have said they'll hook me up but I don't want to experiment till I'm home. Listen, I don't want to hog the phone. There's someone here who needs to talk to you more than me."

"What?"

"See you soon, mate."

A new voice came on, one he knew well. "Hello Alex."

"Hi Becky."

"How are you?"

"Not too bad. You?"

"I'm okay. I think we need to talk about things."

"Yeah …"

"You found out about Roberto from Sarah Sceney?"

"Yeah."

"Listen, the reason I didn't tell you about him is because I wanted to wait and see what happened. I wasn't sure if I liked him or not."

"Has anything happened between you?"

"I'm not going to lie to you, Alex. We've kissed."

Alex's heart sank to the soles of his Dunlop Volleys. "So you're dumping me?"

"Let me finish. After we kissed I knew that I

didn't like him. Well I like him, but not like that. As a friend."

"What?"

"I don't like him the same way I like you."

"Are you sure?"

"Positive."

Alex felt the green-eyed monster rise up in his gut. "But why did you kiss him if you just like him as a friend?"

"Well, it just sort of happened. Have you kissed anyone since I've left?"

"No!" he said. He really believed he was telling the truth, until it struck him that he wasn't. "Yes," he said quietly. "But it's over now."

There was silence for a bit.

"There's something else you should know," she said.

"What?"

"I'm coming back to Brisbane in a month. Mum's going to give Dad another chance."

At that moment Alex and words became strangers.

"Well?" she said. "Say something. Are you happy?"

"Maybe," he said.

"Maybe? What sort of answer is that?"

"Maybe I am and maybe I'm not."

"If you want to keep going out you better say you're happy."

"I'm happy."

They chuckled. "If you were here now I might even have let you kiss me," said Becky.

Alex could hear Casey in the background. "He's not here, so I'll do it for him!"

Alex laughed. "Tell him he's not allowed. Tell him I'll do it myself in a month's time. That is, if it's all right with you?"

"I'll think about it."

CHAPTER 27

Skatey Video

Three months later Alex got the chance to be in a skating video. Not an amateur job either, but a professional one made by the Zen team. The team had asked permission from the Logan City Council to use spots around Beeton, and the mayor thought it would bring good publicity and gave it the all-clear.

Of course it was Casey and the other pros in the team who were the stars, but Alex was given a small but important part. He was going to boardslide the courthouse stairs.

"Five minutes," said the director.

"You know what to do," said Casey. "Trust yourself and your body will find a way."

"How many cameras are there again?" asked Alex.

"Three. But forget about them and the people watching."

Alex looked down at the carpark. The landing area was cordoned off and a number of curious observers stood behind the rope. He could see his mum and Chief watching anxiously. His mum hadn't wanted him to be in the video but Alex talked her into it. "It's no worries, Mum. I can do this trick in my sleep."

He wasn't lying. In his sleep he never missed a trick. It was in real life that he had problems.

Chief was just back from Russia, bringing home strange but interesting presents. Alex received a Russian rap CD and Sam a traditional folk-dancing costume. Chief had an excellent time and loved telling the story of how Ben, behind on points, knocked out the Russian champion right before the final bell.

Jimmy looked up and waved. He said he would build an Alex Jackson web page if Alex weaselled his way onto the Zen video. "I'll only take 50 per cent of the money and 100 per cent of the girls," he said.

John was on Jimmy's left, talking to no one in particular. *Probably rapping.* Alex, John and Jimmy had been hanging out together lately, going to the gym every Friday night for boxing training with Chief. John loved it, even though he had learnt the hard way to keep his hands high when he was popped on the nose sparring. His English was improving, as well as his temper, and he wasn't picked on as much at school.

Sarah was next to John, talking to a friend. Though she was not the same old Sarah, and probably never would be after her dad left, she was one of the group again. She and Jimmy even talked about getting back together (Alex called him a pushover), but they agreed it would be best to be just friends. For now. She was getting A's again — which had to be a good sign. She was happy being smart.

The friend Sarah was talking to was Becky. Being apart for so long made it easy for Alex to see how she had changed. Her curves were more noticeable and she had a hint of red in her long, black hair. Alex could just make out the necklace that hung down to the top of her chest. It was a purple stone in the shape of a heart. He had to smile. He was the luckiest guy in Beeton.

There was another face he knew, right at the back of the crowd. She ducked her head when she saw him look, but it was definitely her. *I wonder if she hopes I'll fall?* He would probably never know, but he had a feeling she wanted him to nail it. Even if she didn't, it made him feel better to think she was on his side.

He remembered something. "Hey Casey," he said, "do you know a boarder called Ryan McTeigue?"

Casey looked sideways at him. "Who told you about him?"

"When you were away I skated with his brother, Steve. He said you two are friends."

"We were. We used to skate around Beeton together, doing crazy stuff and getting into trouble."

"You never told me," said Alex.

"I'm not proud of it."

"Where is he now?"

"Ryan?" asked Casey.

"Yeah."

"You don't know?"

"Know what?"

"Ryan died," he said. "He was hit by a car on his board, skating away from the cops."

Alex was stunned.

"He was an unbelievable skater, better than me, but totally out of control. He had no respect for anyone or anything. It taught me a lesson. I was heading down the same track."

Casey sighed. "What's his brother like?"

"Pretty much the same."

"I'd like to meet him."

"Come back here Friday night."

The director yelled out, "It's time. Everyone in position. Take one."

Take one? If there needed to be a take two he was in big trouble. They might have to film it from the Logan hospital.

Alex Jackson pushed off, felt the rush as he gathered momentum across the smooth slate tiles, and knew once more that all was right with the world.